Warning

Dedication

To the usual suspects, whose love and support make dreaming big seem as natural as breathing.

Acknowledgment

To everyone who has read this book or my others. My writing is truly a labor of love, and I hope you enjoy reading the books as much as I enjoy writing them.

Prologue

The sound of sex was unmistakable. At first Sara thought it was the TV. Nate wasn't expecting her home for a few more hours, and he often watched porn when she wasn't in the house. He refused to admit that he watched, but Sara knew he had a drawer full of skin magazines and DVDs. She was about to call out to him, announcing her presence, when a breathy, feminine voice screamed out his name.

"Harder, Nate. Oh God, harder."

Sara's stomach turned with unease as she came closer to the stairs. When she heard Nate's voice as he grunted, tears burned in her eyes. She didn't have to see it to know. Beyond a doubt her boyfriend was having sex with someone else. In their house, in their bed. She didn't have to look to know it, but the compulsion was more than she could resist.

She made her way up the stairs, stepping carefully to avoid the squeaking spot on the top step. She needn't have bothered trying to be quiet. Nate was too intent on fucking the woman beneath him to notice her standing in the doorway to their bedroom.

Sara waited patiently as he pounded into the fiery redhead, treating her far more passionately than he'd ever been with Sara. She had to admit if it had been anyone but her boyfriend, she would have found the show he was putting on stimulating. Lately their sex life had become stagnant. Sara had figured it was just something that was bound to happen over time. She loved Nate, and she'd assumed it was something that would pass, but watching him now it became painfully obvious that he'd never felt that kind of passion for her.

Chapter One

It was supposed to be an amazing vacation—two weeks away in a secluded cabin in the wilderness where Sara Torres could sort out her next move, get her shit together, and figure out what she was doing with her life. It was supposed to be a chance to relax and recharge, for her to enjoy a quiet Christmas on her own, so she could put her lying, cheating ex-boyfriend behind her and move on. What it was so far was a nightmare. Her car had slid off the road after hitting a patch of ice when she had swerved to avoid the deer darting across the road. The deer had gotten away scot-free—Sara hadn't been so lucky.

Sara pressed her shaking fingers to the ache in her forehead, stunned to come away with blood. It wasn't a lot of blood, she thought, trying to console herself and maintain some small measure of calm.

Her vision blurred, and she squeezed her eyes shut, trying to force them back into focus. She cursed Nate for the millionth time since finding him with another woman.

She couldn't just sit here. Her car couldn't be seen from the road, and with snow falling, evidence that her car went off the road would soon be obscured. There was no way she could drive her car back up the steep embankment. She would have to get back to the road to flag down help. Sara put her shoulder into the door, pushing against the mangled frame when the door didn't open effortlessly. It took a few shoves, but finally the door creaked open.

Cold air whipped into the interior of her tiny, beat-up car, making Sara's teeth chatter. The coat she was wearing wasn't much of a match for the wind, but she'd left her heavier jacket at home, not wanting to face Nate to go back for it. She had rationalized that with layers, she'd be all right without it. Now, shivering and exposed to the elements, she regretted that decision.

Struggling out of the car, she cringed when icy, wet snow spilled over the top of her calf-high boot and soaked her left foot. She placed her right foot more gingerly, careful to avoid sending more of the nearly knee-deep snow down her boots.

Looking up at the embankment, Sara let out a cry of dismay. It was too steep to climb here. For the first time since leaving she wished she'd brought her cell phone, but repeated pleading calls from Nate had made her leave it behind. Muttering a soft curse beneath her breath, Sara started walking in an attempt to find an area that looked easier to climb.

* * * *

He'd been tracking the deer when she darted for the road. Jace had been intently following her, but the snow was coming down much harder than it had an hour ago. He was about to turn back to his cabin but then an unfamiliar scent drifted to him on the wind. A soft, feminine, slightly floral scent that had no place in the dead of winter, it made his interest flare even in his animal form. He felt his dick pulse with the rush of unexpected blood as desire kicked him in the gut.

He sighed, and the movement translated to his wolf huffing with a toss of his big head. Jace could think like a man in this form, but his thoughts were centered on more animalistic needs. The desire for sex and violence was prevalent, and it had been too long since he had taken a woman. The closest lycan pack was miles away. Not wanting to submit to another alpha, and not wanting to challenge to rule the pack he'd grown up in, Jace chose to live alone.

The floral scent was stronger now as he doubled back to where the deer had made her escape. He came upon an old clunker of a car covered in a few inches of snow. The pungent smell of fear and pain was still thick. The floral scent was present too and under that the copper tang of blood. The combination of the feminine aroma mixed with blood made the wolf angry, and Jace had to clamp down on the violent emotions to keep his mind reacting as a human would.

He pressed his muzzle in the snow, dragging the smell into his lungs and imprinting it on his brain. He followed the trail away from the car. Any tracks that had been made in the snow were long gone.

Nearly an hour passed before Jace stumbled upon her lying facedown in the snow. As it was, only the dark fabric of her coat and his good sense of smell alerted him to her presence. He would have thought her dead if the sensitive hearing of the wolf hadn't been able to pick up the thud of her heart. Though it was frighteningly sluggish, it made him hopeful that he'd found her in time and that she'd be all right.

* * * *

Jace placed her gently on his bed, thankful that she hadn't stirred while he carried her back to his cabin. It would have been difficult to explain why he was naked and carrying her off to his home. She hadn't moved at all when he shifted or when he carefully looked her over for injuries before lifting her limp body and rushing back to the cabin. In his animal form, he didn't feel the cold, but even though he felt the cold less as a human, he still needed to get back quickly.

Jace rushed to pull on a faded pair of sweatpants, cursing the sensitivity that lingered on his skin. He had forced the change, and his body would rebel soon, demanding that he rest, but he had to know that she was all right first.

If she was seriously injured, he would need to find a way to get her medical attention, but the storm rolling in would make the roads impassable.

Jace hurriedly stripped off her jacket, careful to avoid jarring her body in case he had missed an injury. He removed her boots, marveling at her delicate feet. They seemed so small, he mused as he rolled down her wet socks and replaced them with a pair of his own thicker, heavier socks. He struggled with her jeans, the wet denim clinging to her cool skin. Once they came loose, he tossed them to the floor, where they landed with a heavy, wet *thump*. Then he checked her legs for any signs of broken bones and smiled, relieved, when everything seemed fine. He cringed when he removed her soft, cream-colored sweater and an ugly purple bruise was revealed. The long contusion spread from her shoulder across her collarbone and chest, obviously from the bite of the seat belt when she went off the road.

A low rumble escaped his throat as he battled the anger seeing her small frame battered had ignited in him. He cursed the damn deer and himself, knowing that ultimately he, or rather his wolf, was the reason the deer had sprung out in front of her car.

Jace quickly examined her upper body for injuries other than the bruise marring her flesh. He pushed away the attraction he felt toward her, surprised to find that it was difficult to ignore the temptation of her exposed skin, even with his medical training. Thankful that her underwear had been dry enough to leave on, he dressed her in the matching sweatshirt to the pants he was wearing. With that task complete, he tucked her beneath the blankets and turned his attention to her head wound. There was dried blood on her forehead. It was caked into her mahogany-colored hair, darkening it to nearly black.

Jace filled a large bowl with warm water and cleaned the wound, careful to be as gentle as possible. Once the dried blood was cleaned away, the shallow gash in her hairline became visible. It began seeping blood again, and Jace found himself fighting the urge to lap at the spilling blood.

"Get a grip, man!" he scolded himself as he smeared antiseptic gel on the wound and pressed a thick white bandage to her forehead. He didn't think the gash would need to be stitched, but he would have to keep an eye on it.

With his medical training, he could do it if she did need stitches, but he didn't have anything on hand to numb her skin while he sewed the torn flesh together. The thought of harming her made his stomach roll.

She shivered, and Jace stoked the dying fire back to life, shaking himself as fatigue from the change pulled at him. He eyed his bed with a forlorn glance and, suppressing his desire to curl up next to his unexpected guest, he set the alarm on his phone to wake him in a few hours so he could check on her and then lay down on the thick rug in front of the hearth in case she needed him.

Chapter Two

The wind howled against the wooden logs of the cabin's walls, rattling the windowpanes. Jace rose and stretched, wishing that he was more refreshed. He'd checked her wounds several times during the night, carefully watching for signs that they were worsening or that a fever was spiking. He shook his head, trying to clear the last of the cobwebs that rapid shifting made cling to his kind. He was strong and able to shift at will, but as strong as he was, even he couldn't escape all of the effects of shifting. Not allowing his body the rest that it needed following a change left his mind foggy and his body on edge.

The skin sensitivity that followed his change had faded, and he felt normal now. His stomach gave a long, low rumble, reminding him of the necessity of food following the transformation. He was ravenous. It came with the territory of being a wolf. He'd become accustomed to the persistent hunger pains that had plagued him since puberty, when he'd first shifted.

Jace checked on the woman in his bed, unable to keep his distance. There was simply something about her that called to him on a primal level. Unable to stop himself, he brushed his hand across her forehead and down her cheek, careful to avoid the bandage.

He rationalized away his movement as checking for fever as he had throughout the night, but he knew he was lying to himself. She did feel warm, though, and Jace was glad he'd given in to his need to touch her.

She whimpered softly, shifting restlessly under the blankets. He hushed her, murmuring in a low, soothing tone, and she quieted almost instantly. He stood over her, unable to tear his gaze away, but when his stomach gave another insistent growl, he reluctantly left the room to find them both food.

He heated a large pot of stew on the stove before making his way over to the phone. He lifted the receiver to his ear, but there was no dial tone. Jace hung up and went back to preparing their meal, and he was cutting thick slices of homemade bread when he heard her in the bedroom.

Her breathing had changed, and there was a small yelp of pain or panic—it was impossible to tell which. Then her heart began racing.

Leaving the bread on the large wooden cutting block, he made his way back to his bedroom in time to see her struggling to leave his bed.

"Whoa, easy there," he cautioned gently, coming close enough to help her if she needed.

"Where am I?" Her voice rasped out, accompanied by a hacking cough.

Jace darted back out to the kitchen for water.

She was still in the bed when he returned. Having given up on trying to push off the blankets, she sat half propped against his pillows and was eyeing him with a distinct lack of trust in her eyes.

"Water," he said, offering the glass. He waited while she stared at it, clearly battling with whether or not to accept it. "It's just water, I promise." Jace brought the glass to his own lips and took a drink before offering it to her again. He was rewarded with a small, trembling smile, and his wolf beamed at having provided for her and having won a small level of her trust.

She reached out for the glass, and their fingers brushed. It was like being hit by a bolt of lightning. Every nerve ending in his body came alive, spreading rapidly from that slight touch. Did she feel it too? His inner wolf perked up, paying closer attention to her reactions.

Jace watched as a flush spread up her neck and bloomed in her cheeks. Her breathing was heavier, and she refused to meet his gaze. *She must have felt it too.*

SARA TOOK THE glass with shaking fingers and swallowed a mouthful carefully. The cool liquid soothed her throat, and she tried to speak again.

"Where am I? What happened?" She could recall nearly hitting the deer and spinning off the road, but anything after that was a bit fuzzy.

"I found you in the snow and brought you here to my home. I'm Jace Wilde." The man offered her his hand, and Sara stared at it for a moment, almost afraid to touch him again, overwhelmed by the intense reaction she'd had to him the first time their fingers brushed against each other.

He was incredibly handsome, his dark hair curling in waves around his ears. His jawline was strong. His lips were wide, and she had the strangest urge to run her fingers along their seam to see if they were as soft as they looked. She'd like to feel them on her skin. The thought came out of nowhere, and as she felt her nipples pull tight, she was glad for the thick covering of blankets. It was his eyes that captivated her though.

She'd never seen another pair of eyes like his. They were steel gray with glints that looked like sterling silver running in their depths. Flecks of charcoal black swirled there too, melting into the darkest pupil she'd ever seen.

Realizing that she'd been staring, she took his offered hand. It was no different than when they'd brushed fingertips when she'd taken the glass. Heat zinged from her palm up her arm, making her flush hot with sudden desire. Trying desperately to ignore the instantaneous lust that assaulted her, she shook his hand briefly before tugging her hand back and offering her own name.

"Sara, Sara Torres. Thank you for helping me."

"The pleasure was all mine, Sara."

The way his voice caressed her name made her tremble. She leaned in closer to him without even realizing it. Their lips were only inches apart. They were too close for two people who were strangers, but that urge to kiss him, to feel his mouth on her own, was stronger than anything she'd ever felt before.

Her stomach rumbled, and his reciprocated in kind, breaking the spell that was weaving between them.

JACE PULLED BACK, a smile filled with regret curving his lips. Lord, how he wanted this woman. The need he felt was stronger than any he'd ever experienced before, and his wolf egged him on. He'd been seconds from claiming her lips, and he knew the way his wolf was behaving he wouldn't have stopped there. *Mate.*

The wolf knew what he wanted, but Jace was stunned. Humans and shifters could have sex — there was no reason that they couldn't — but mate? That was a different thing entirely, and as far as he knew, it wasn't done. Even with the number of female shifters dwindling, a mating between a shifter and human would be considered taboo.

Chapter Three

The bowl of stew he placed on her lap smelled delicious. The bed tray also held another glass of water and bread with butter. She'd been hungry, and he'd only been gone for a few minutes to retrieve the food, but now her appetite was gone.

"Sara, please, you really should try to eat something," he said.

Sara could feel his gaze on her, and it felt disapproving. In the time that she'd been toying with her spoon and staring at her food, he'd finished two bowls and was working on his third.

The stew was a rich broth with chunks of beef and onions, carrots, and potatoes. It smelled good, but she was simply no longer hungry.

"I'm sorry. I don't think I can." Her head was pounding now, and she wanted to lie back down. She watched wearily as Jace came and sat on the edge of the bed.

"Here, let me help you." Jace took the spoon from the bowl and brought it to her lips. His movements were natural, as if he'd done this a hundred times before. Embarrassment over being spoon-fed by a virtual stranger flared to life, but with his help she was able to slide down in the bed slightly, and the throbbing in her head eased.

She parted her lips, and he deposited the food into her mouth as gently as he would if she were a baby. The thought made her instantly nervous, and her gaze flew to his hands in search of a wedding ring.

Not finding one, she relaxed slightly, but it was possible he was married and didn't have a ring. Or wasn't married but had children anyway. Jace fed her another bite and another. All the while her mind was a mass of turmoil. When he put the spoon down for the last time, a horrible thought occurred to her.

"Um, whose bed is this?" Sara hated that her voice came out weak, but if he was married, she was getting up out of bed immediately, whether she was hurt or not.

"It's my bed, Sara." He paused, making sure she was looking straight at him. "Only my bed." He reassured her as if he'd sensed her discomfort.

His answer gave her a small measure of relief, and she let out the breath she hadn't realized she'd been holding.

"Jace, do you have any aspirin? My head is killing me."

"Of course. It's in the bathroom." He paused and cast her an embarrassed look. "Do you need to go? I can help you up or bring you something to use if that's easier."

Sara laughed, more from mutual embarrassment and humiliation than from humor. "My back hurts and my head feels like it might explode, but I think I can manage."

He moved the tray from her lap and helped her push back the covers. Sara gave a startled gasp as her bare legs were revealed. Her shocked gaze flew to his.

"You were soaked from head to toe. I wanted you warm as quickly as possible." He seemed to flush under his tanned complexion, but he looked so sincere, never taking his gaze off her, that Sara felt her outrage melt away. She could see her jeans and sweater drying over the back of a chair by the fire, and she still had her bra and panties on, so it was clear he hadn't removed more than what was necessary. The fact that his gaze didn't stray from her face when her legs were exposed helped reassure her of his noble intentions.

JACE WATCHED AS she swung her legs around to the side of the bed, her movements stilted by the pain in her body. He was thrilled in that moment that he had something to offer her for the pain.

Normally he didn't bother keeping much on hand. His metabolism worked so quickly that most medication didn't faze him, but it would help her, and for that he was grateful. Comforting her, making her happy, and protecting her seemed to be becoming one of his top priorities, making his wolf preen.

She stood on wobbly legs, and the scent of her desire hit him hard. He had managed to clamp down on his control, tightly reigning in his reactions to her, but one whiff of the evidence of her lust, of her reaction to him, and he wanted to sink to his knees in front of her and lap it all up until he made her spill more.

It was driving his wolf near to madness, and he felt the brush of fur though his body as he fought the push of his wolf. *NO!* He screamed the word in his mind, imagining a steel cage to hold the wolf, and that part of him snarled his displeasure before quieting again.

Jace watched as she struggled, every instinct he possessed screaming from him to wrap his arm around her waist and help her over to the bathroom. As it was, he hovered close in case she needed him. He heaved a sigh of relief when she closed the door behind her, muting the scent of her arousal.

Despite his desire to leave the room for a few minutes to compose himself, Jace couldn't move away from the door. Fearful that she'd need him, he stayed glued to the spot. He could hear the pep talk she gave herself on the other side of the door, believing that her voice was low enough to avoid being overheard.

Her dialogue was so similar to his own thoughts that he wanted to laugh at the absurdity of their situation.

"He's just a good-looking guy. Just another pretty face, Sara. Get ahold of yourself. You are not doing this. You need to get out of here. He could be an axe murderer, for crying out loud." She blew out a sigh, and the water started running in the sink, making it harder for Jace to catch her words. "It doesn't matter anyway how much you want — not after Nate. Not again."

Jace stiffened at the mention of another man's name, surprised as jealousy bloomed to life inside him over the faceless rival. *MATE!* He felt his jaw ache, signaling the coming of fangs rather than human teeth, and clenched his teeth together until he thought they might crack.

The bathroom door creaked open, and Sara hung limply in the doorway, her strength having waned since leaving the bed. Any anger or envy he'd felt fled, and his desire to protect and provide for Sara surged to the forefront again.

"Here, let me help you back to bed." She gave a small nod, and he took her weight against his own. "We should check your bandage. I think your wound might still be bleeding. You're weaker than I'd like to see you, given you've eaten and rested." Seeing her struggle even with his support, Jace scooped her into her arms as if she weighed nothing and crossed the small distance to the bed. He'd set her down on the mattress and settled the blankets around her again before she'd even had the chance to protest.

Seeing that she was going to try anyway, he placed his fingers against her lips, halting the words he could see dying to spill out. "You're tired. Helping you was faster. I couldn't let you expend energy you need to heal." She nodded her understanding, causing Jace to smile. Her lips were like velvet under his fingers, and he couldn't resist a gentle caress before pulling away.

Regaining his composure, he carefully removed the bandage at her forehead. The gash was still seeping blood, and the metallic tang was sweet. He licked his lips in what he hoped appeared to be concentration rather than hunger. "I wish this had stopped bleeding," he said, and there was a genuine pang of regret in his tone. The bleeding had slowed, and for that much he was grateful. It made the call of the blood easier to resist.

"I don't think it will need stitches. I hope it won't, because I don't have the supplies to do that here and the storm has gotten worse while we slept." As if to prove his point, the wind kicked up and snow pelted against the window, battering at the cabin.

"You could do that? Put in stitches?" He could smell the fear that laced her question.

"I have medical training. I've worked as a paramedic. If I needed to, I could perform a number of medical procedures, including setting broken bones or stitching the wound in your hairline. I just don't have anything to numb the skin. It would hurt, and I don't want to cause you pain."

Jace grabbed her glass from the nightstand and refilled it from the bathroom sink. When he came back into the room, he handed her the glass and a couple of aspirins.

* * * *

Sara dreamed of wolves. It wasn't the first time that she had, but this dream was stranger than all the others. In this dream, the wolf found her in the snow and rescued her, but in this dream the wolf had eyes the color of Jace's, and he watched her with intelligence. He padded over to her on nearly silent feet. He sat in front of her as if seeking permission and then nudged her leg with his muzzle. The feeling of soft fur against her naked flesh made her shudder, and she could feel hot, wet arousal slide from her body to coat her thighs. His tongue caressed her from knee to midthigh in a calculated, sensual movement.

Her knees trembled, and longing curled within her belly. Giving up all resistance, Sara let her knees fall open. There was a look of triumph in his eyes as he leaned forward. Human lips kissed her pubic mound before his tongue delved into her depths. His lips firmed around her clit, creating suction so tantalizing she cried out his name, screaming her climax as the last syllable rang out.

Chapter Four

Sara came awake with a jolt, her heart pounding and chest heaving. Had she really called out his name? She had to get out of here. She felt like she was slowly going insane. Sara had had wolf dreams before but never something erotic like what she'd just experienced. Most of the time she dreamed of running wild, and in the dream she was a wolf or with wolves, but she'd never had sex with one.

Well, to be accurate, the wolf had been Jace. God, the man was dangerous. She'd known him for only a few hours, yet somehow she was ready to sleep with him. Mate, she thought suddenly and blushed at how furiously she wanted him.

He didn't come rushing into the room, so she assumed she hadn't called out for him after all. *Thank God for small favors.* She could feel the wetness from her orgasm against the inside of her thighs and gathered along the folds of her sex.

She still felt sensitive, and the dream cane back to her unbidden.

Sara groaned, burying her head in her hands, then winced with the pain the action brought. "Damn it!" she cursed, hot tears burning in her eyes and making her throat tight.

She was getting out of the bed when Jace came through the door. He came to her side immediately, offering assistance, and it made her want to cry harder. She'd been with Nate for almost four years, and he hadn't been a tenth as attentive as Jace had been in the hours since they met.

"Hey, hey, what's wrong?" His gentle tone made her bury her face in his chest and sob.

"I'm sorry. It's just been a really horrible day. Do you think you could take me back into the nearest town so I can get out of here?"

Jace stroked her hair. "I would, Sara, but the storm has gotten a lot worse since I found you. I barely made it back from your car just now when I went to get your things. There's no way we'd make it to the road until the storm lets up."

Sara couldn't stop her gasp of shock. Was it possible he was telling the truth? As she listened to the weather raging outside, she was almost afraid to look out the window. She pushed back the covers and got out of bed to move closer to the window. She pulled back the heavy drape and wished she hadn't. It was like being trapped inside a snow globe that someone kept turning over. She could feel the cold pressing against the glass. She shivered and let the heavy fabric fall back into place, blocking out the majority of the cold.

"I guess you're stuck with me."

THE LOOK SHE gave him was so sad, he nearly kissed her to obliterate it from his mind. *Mate.* The word whispered though his mind again, and he fought to ignore it and the pressing need to have her.

"I'm going to go get more wood," Jace announced before fleeing the confines of the cabin.

Once he was outside and could breathe easier, he admitted that running from her wasn't a very alpha thing to do, but his wolf couldn't stand being around her any longer without taking her, and he wouldn't do that without her permission. It had only been two days, and while his kind formed deep attachments to their partners quickly, he knew it was frightening for humans to feel that much for each other that rapidly.

Jace wanted to shift. His wolf was pressing for freedom, the desire to mate or run riding him hard. Since he couldn't shift and run without the risk of being discovered, Jace began splitting firewood, hoping that the exertion would quiet the animal raging inside him.

He buried himself in the manual labor, trying to ignore how much he wanted her. He wouldn't have sex with a human. It wasn't to protect some idealistic idea about the purity of lycan bloodlines the way some of his brethren were. He simply wouldn't fuck a human because, in his opinion, they were far too fragile. It didn't stop him from wanting to though.

When she had called out his name earlier, her arousal thick and perfuming his bedroom, it was all he could do not to storm into the room and take her. Just thinking about it made the blood pulse in his veins and made splitting the logs pointless.

* * * *

"I hope you don't mind, but I went through the freezer and found something to eat." Sara stirred the pot on the stove as Jace set the table. "I was feeling a bit better and started going stir crazy just lying around." When he'd first rescued her, Sara had spent most days sleeping as her injuries began to heal, but now that she'd been on the mend for nearly a week, she felt stronger and was anxious to make herself useful.

"No, it's fine. Thank you. I'm starving. I'm just not used to having someone around for things like that."

They ate in easy silence. It was so comfortable that it amazed Sara. She had never felt that comfortable with Nate. Looking back now, she could recognize how strained their relationship had become. It was probably at least part of what had driven him to cheat.

Thinking about it made her chest tight. Sara rubbed absently at the physical ache the memory caused. She was surprised when Jace reached for her other hand. Again the electricity arched between them. It made her gasp with its intensity.

"So, you do feel it too, then," Jace said, caressing the back of her hand gently.

Sara could only nod as the simple touch seared her nerve endings.

"I have spent all day trying to convince myself that it's wrong to want you." Jace whispered the words. He pulled his hand back from hers, and Sara felt his absence acutely.

"We barely know each other," she whispered, wishing he'd take her hand again. She wasn't sure if it was because he'd saved her from freezing to death or if it was simply that he was an attractive and virile man and she was hurt and lonely from Nate's betrayal.

"This is a really bad storm. One weather system barely has time to let up before the next one rolls through. Sara, where were you going before I found you?"

Jace had asked her just after rescuing her, but Sara had deflected his line of questioning, Nate's betrayal too fresh. Now the abrupt change in conversation from something deep and meaningful to something as mundane as the weather felt like a slap in the face. Sara felt heat crawl into her cheeks and tried to ignore the sting that his rejection caused her.

"I was headed to a cabin in the area off Clear Creek Lake. I'd planned to stay a few weeks."

"I know the cabin. It's a few miles north of here. It's pretty rustic—how were you planning to occupy your time?"

"I brought my camera with me. The scenery is supposed to be great up that way, and I was hoping to get some good wildlife photos. And I have my e-reader with me. I wasn't really looking for a lot of entertainment. I just wanted to relax."

"So close to Christmas?"

"I didn't feel much like celebrating this year. I just needed to get away."

"There will be even more snow there than what we have here, and we've had a lot. Probably about two and a half feet since this morning. Freezing rain was starting when I was coming back from your car. I'm glad I went when I did, or I'd never have gotten the doors open. I tried to call the sheriff the day I found you, but the phone was already out. I left a note on the front seat so if someone reported seeing your car, he'd know where you were, but it will be a bit before it's safe to leave here."

"So you really are stuck with me, then."

"Yeah, for at least a few more days anyway." Jace chuckled, trying to lighten the mood. "But if the weather lets up a bit, maybe you can still get some good pictures. The scenery is pretty great around here too."

* * * *

When they did the dishes together, Jace realized they went out of their way to touch each other. It was so subtle that he doubted Sara even realized it, but they stood, hips and legs bumping into each other while their hands and arms brushed up against each other when reaching into the dish rack.

Jace studied her out of the corner of his eye, his enhanced senses making the covert job much easier. He had taken the time to study her earlier when she'd been unconscious, but that had been more from a medical-status standpoint. He hadn't been able to see her eyes then either, and he knew now why he'd felt so deprived at the time. They were a rich honey-amber color that reminded him of eyes he'd seen at pack gatherings.

Her eyes were so similar to shifter eyes that he'd taken a long whiff of her, drawing her essence deep into his lungs and testing her fragrance the way he'd sample wine. She wasn't a shifter, he was sure of it. His kind could always sense one another, even if they weren't the same breed of shifter. Yet something in the depths of her eyes still compelled him to verify that she was completely human.

Chapter Five

After dinner Sara curled up on the couch with her e-reader but soon found that trying to read from the screen made her head pound. She fingered the edge of the bandage and cursed the continued weakness that came and went. *Some vacation this turned out to be, Sara.*

She felt the hot burn of tears that her humiliation brought, but refusing to let them fall, she scrunched her eyes closed.

"I'll read to you if you want," Jace offered, and before she could stop him, he had her e-reader in his hands.

"No, no, that's all right. Here, give me that. You don't have to do that." She reached for the book, but Jace held it away from her. "Really, I appreciate the offer, but it's not necessary." Sara reached for the e-reader again, but tangled in the throw blanket she had curled up under, she wasn't nearly quick enough to snatch it from his hands.

Sara tried to remember how graphic the passage she'd been reading was, and humiliation swamped her. It was pretty graphic, and having a man like Jace read something like that to her would definitely send her hormones into overdrive.

She watched as one of his eyebrows rose in a perfect arch over those eyes she was mesmerized by. She tried once more to stop him before he started reading.

The deep timber of his tone made her shiver as reading the sensual words on her own never had. She watched his lips form the words, fantasizing about his lips and tongue as she caught glimpses of it against his teeth.

He looked up from the reader and caught her staring at him. It made her hold her breath, but she couldn't look away.

"Pretty hot stuff you're reading, Sara," he said, and his words made her cheeks heat further.

"I told you not to read it," she snapped defiantly, and then in a voice barely above a whisper, she said, "You can pick something else." She could feel her ears heating while she refused to meet his gaze.

"Oh no, I think this is a fine selection."

Her head whipped back in his direction so quickly that it made her heart pound in her temples. Their gazes locked, and Jace shot her a teasing smile before resuming his reading.

JACE FELT HIS own pulse race when he realized that the very sensual, racy novel had a paranormal theme. The passage he read from now had the hero taking the heroine to her knees in the forest and mounting her.

Jace had to admit the scene was hot and was at least somewhat accurate in depicting what he and his wolf wanted to do to Sara.

Sara... God she was stunning, her breath coming faster when he read something she found particularly stimulating, and all the while her gaze never left him. He could almost imagine those honeyed eyes staring up at him as he thrust into her soft, welcoming pussy.

He let the e-reader fall to his lap, unable to continue torturing himself. Shifting the topic to something other than sex, he asked, "So, wolves, huh?" Jace watched her raise her shoulder in a careless shrug. "A little hokey, don't you think?" he questioned her again, needing to press for an answer. She gave another half shrug, but he could sense the embarrassment unfurling inside her as she picked her words carefully.

"It's just fantasy. All of it, really. Prince Charming doesn't ride in on a white horse and rescue the damsel in distress, and consuming need like the passage you just read— well, there is a reason it's called fiction." There was an emotion burning in her eyes that even his enhanced senses couldn't describe when she continued. "Trust me. In real life, our unsuspecting heroine walks in on Prince Charming, only to find him balls-deep in some other woman, and it turns out that he's a toad not even worth having kissed in the first place. Worse still, he's a rat-bastard who tries to explain his behavior away because—because..." Her words died off, and her humiliation hung between them a sour note on the back of his tongue.

"She just hadn't met the right prince yet, and to set the record straight, I wasn't on horseback, white or otherwise, when I swooped in to rescue you."

"I guess you really did save me," Sara whispered, and before Jace could stop her, she leaned in and kissed him. It was a chaste kiss meant to express gratitude rather than to provoke his lust, but it rocked the very core of his being.

* * * *

Jace stayed on the couch long after Sara had turned in for the night, guilt eating at him. If he hadn't been hunting, the deer wouldn't have caused her accident, and Sara would never have needed him to rescue her.

He couldn't regret the circumstances that brought them together though. With fewer female shifters being born each year, finding a mate was increasingly difficult. The reason for the decline wasn't fully known. It had started slowly, and many of their scientists believed it to be naturally occurring genetics. They were testing their theories, but until further blood and DNA analysis could be done, the wolf council didn't have any solid answers. Jace punched at the pillow on the couch, trying to curve his body into a comfortable position. He couldn't kick her out of his bed, but he couldn't very well curl up at the foot of the bed the way he had when he first brought her home with him. Could he? If he could ask Ryan about his predicament with Sara, he would, but he wouldn't contact his brother. He wouldn't risk causing the fight he'd left to avoid. They couldn't both be alpha, and Jace refused to kill or even to hurt his brother to claim the spot he wanted for himself in the pack. Caleb's face flashed through his mind, taunting him. Reminding him that he couldn't convincingly lie to himself. His brother wasn't the only reason that he couldn't risk going back to the pack.

The phone rang, and Jace knew before he picked it up that it was Ryan. He smiled and snatched the phone off the cradle, not wanting to wake Sara.

"If you're going to stop acknowledging my existence because of some misguided notion of pride or family honor or some other bullshit, then stop thinking about me so goddamn hard while I'm trying to sleep." His brother's voice rumbled on the other end of the line, and even at this distance, Jace could feel his brother's power.

"It's not misguided." Jace sighed, fearing they were about to go down the same road they'd been on for years now.

"Shut up, asshole. What's wrong?" Ryan asked, reverting to their crass childhood behavior and name-calling. Refusing to acknowledge the rift between them.

Jace ignored the insult. "Do you believe in all the hype about bond mates? Or do you think it's bullshit?"

Ryan heaved a big sigh, and Jace listened to the dead air on the phone. For several minutes, all that could be heard was the gentle rasp of Ryan's breath as it fanned over the mouthpiece of the phone.

"It's not BS. It's the real deal," Ryan said finally, and Jace could feel the hurt roll off his brother in waves with those two simple admissions.

"You're sure? How do you know?" Jace feared for a second that while he'd been in his self-imposed exile, his brother had mated.

"Hayley."

"You've mated?" Jace couldn't keep the excitement from his voice.

"No, but I love her. *Loved* her. I would have mated with her in a heartbeat. Hell, I thought we *had* mated. We were at Eclipse one night having a few beers, and in walks this wolf from another pack. Passing through town, or so he said. He said he didn't want trouble. There was the regular posturing shit, but nothing too outrageous. Next thing you know, dude's got my girl against a wall in the back hallway, practically fucking her in a room full of wolves, and well, the rest is history. I would have beat him for touching her, but Hayley begged me to leave him alone, and just like that she wasn't mine anymore. She was his. They had bonded," Ryan finished on a sad note.

"Could it have just been Hayley's heat?" Jace asked. Female shifters often suffered when they went into heat. The urge to fuck could become unbearable if denied too long and could cause the afflicted female to do desperate things to find relief.

"Nope, this wasn't the same. As soon as she laid eyes on the guy, she went squirrely, and he zeroed in on her like she was the only wolf on the planet."

"Shit."

"Yeah, shit. Anyway, that was about six months ago. The pack is all in an uproar. I had to gain back ground for not fighting the prick. I beat down three challenges. Everyone assumed Hayley was alpha female. Now they know she's not, and all the single females are lining up to 'audition' or something. Hayley's long gone, joined to this wolf and his pack. The council is upset and have doubled their testing. With so few women, it's a blow to us all that she's gone, and that more than anything probably prompted some of the hostility within the pack, but as long as I don't think too hard about her absence, I'm getting by."

"I'm sorry, Rye. Three challenges must have been rough. Who was it?"

"Daniel, Mac, and Aaron. Mac almost had me, but I came out on top. So why are you asking about mating?" Ryan asked casually, brushing aside the fact that he had killed three pack members to maintain his alpha status. Jace felt a momentary stab of remorse for the loss of the men he'd known since boyhood, but violence was inherent in their culture, and if Ryan had shown leniency with any of them, he'd be the one who was dead now.

"Do you think it could happen with a nonshifter?" Jace asked, barely above a whisper, afraid of Ryan's answer.

"What? I don't know. Maybe? There aren't a lot of packs with human members or half-wolf members. I know it hasn't happened in ours, but when you take alpha, certain things are shared that regular pack members aren't privy to. So I do know there have been a few. Why? What's going on, Jace? Come on, man, I'm your older brother, damn it! Put aside all the wolf posturing bullshit, and tell me what's going on."

Jace scoffed. "You are only my older brother by three and a half minutes. Stop trying to mother-hen me." Jace laughed before letting out a dejected sigh. He reminded himself that he'd wanted to talk to Ryan so badly he'd accidentally triggered the mental bond they shared as twin littermates.

He took a deep breath, gathering his courage, then proceeded to tell Ryan about Sara. "I think she's feeling the same way. We can barely keep our hands to ourselves, and man, the scent of her arousal is driving me crazy. I can't get her out of here. There's a bad storm. I'm surprised you even got through on the phone. Service was out all day yesterday. The storm has made things impassable for at least a few days, if not longer. Frankly, I'm running out of reasons why I should stay away from her."

Ryan was quiet for a long time, and Jace thought he wouldn't say anything else, but then he finally spoke.

"I think you're screwed, brother. That is exactly what happened with Hayley."

"Should I mate her? I mean, she's human. Fully human. How do you tell someone 'Hey, I'm a wolf. It's genetic, but hey, don't sweat it 'cause you're my mate and I'm going to take care of you for the rest of our lives—right after I screw the hell out of you'?"

Ryan chuckled, and Jace felt a pang of longing spike him hard in the chest. He missed his family. He wanted to ask about his mother and sister, but he couldn't stand the thought of opening that floodgate.

"I don't think it matters what you say. If she is your mate, then it will happen unless you find a way to get her the hell away from you, but why the hell would you want to, man?"

Caleb's image taunted him again, and he knew Ryan would be aware of his reason for not pursuing Sara, but he couldn't bring himself to suggest it. It was still too painful. "I gotta go, Ryan. Thanks for calling. I'll work harder to keep the mental spillage to a minimum," he promised and disconnected the phone before Ryan could say anything else. A few minutes later, pain sizzled down his spine as Ryan took advantage of their mental bond to punish Jace for his bad manners.

Chapter Six

The sound of her low whine woke him, and instantly every protective instinct inside him burst to awareness. Sara whimpered, and Jace was in his room by her side before she could make another sound.

He expected pain, or maybe fear, when he entered the room, but what greeted him was the strongest scent of desire he'd ever smelled coming from a woman. The scent was rich, earthy, and seductive. It punched him right in the groin. She twisted on the bed, her body contorting in ways Jace hadn't expected from someone human.

"It hurts," she moaned, staring up at him with a dark, imploring gaze, and in that moment Jace felt helpless. He would have done anything to make her pain subside.

He sat on the edge of the bed, careful to avoid jarring her unnecessarily. He felt her brow, his medical training urging him to find something physically wrong with her, something that he could fix.

"Do something. Please, Jace, help me." Sara writhed on the bed. "God, it hurts! It feels like my skin is too tight for my body."

What she was describing sounded very much like the first time Jace ever experienced the change, and he worried that she was going through something similar, but it also sounded like when a female shifter went into their first heat. The combination scared him and had his wolf going in circles with the need to end her misery.

Was it possible that she had possessed shifter DNA? An ancestor in her lineage who was a wolf or some other type of shifter? Or were the changes happening within her something to do with their growing attraction?

She cried out again that it hurt and dug at the pajamas covering her, and he put the intriguing thoughts aside to take action to help her. Moving quickly, he removed her clothing without even pausing to glance at her nakedness. He was only pleased that removing the clothing seemed to give her at least momentary peace, but before long the pain was back and Sara was panting.

"I don't know how to fix this, Sara. I don't even know what's wrong." Desperation colored his tone.

"Kiss me," Sara begged, and Jace stared at her, frozen with indecision. "Please, I'm going crazy here." Jace shook his head slowly, ready to deny her again, but she whimpered pleading with him again. "Please, Jace, this need—it's tearing me apart." She ran her hands over her body as she begged him again, and his wolf wouldn't allow him to delay any longer. Their mate needed them, and if the man wouldn't cooperate willingly, the wolf would make him. Sharp teeth and claws seemed to rake through his insides, spurring him to action.

He slanted his mouth over hers, sealing them together. It was everything the chaste kiss was not, and it fuelled their passion for each other.

JACE'S KISS WAS like no other man's. He kissed her like he owned her, and she reveled in it. She savored his kiss, enjoying the finer nuances even in their frenzy. His kiss was like balm on the fire racing through her veins. She kissed him until her lips felt bruised and swollen, again and again until her heart pounded heavily in her chest and her lungs demanded air. Only then did she tear her lips away from his, breathing heavily.

The ache she felt dissipated slightly, and she lay panting while the burn slowly built again. She rolled her head across the pillow to look at him. "Jace." It was all she could manage before she needed him to kiss her again. She felt like an addict, and fear raced through her, momentarily obliterating the lust.

"I know, sweetheart. It's getting bad for me too." As if to emphasize his point, he pressed the hard ridge of his erection against her thigh, and Sara could feel it pulse behind the cloth of his pants.

"I need you." She cried out again, arching into his touch as he ground down against her. It had never felt like this for Sara. The few guys she'd slept with in college and since had felt wrong, their touch turning her body cold.

"Sara, if I take my pants off, I don't think I'll be able to stop. I don't want to do anything you don't want me to do." The strain was evident in his voice as he fought his response to her.

"Jace, I'm not saying no here," she whined.

He looked to the ceiling, as if seeking divine guidance or intervention, before he bit out a violent curse.

Jace brushed her hands out of his way and palmed her breasts. The feel of his work-roughened, calloused fingers against the tender flesh of her breasts made her groan. When he thumbed the turgid peaks, she sighed with relief, then moaned as pleasure swamped her system.

He kissed her again before sliding his mouth along her cheek, dropping kisses along her jawline and down her throat. Sara arched and offered him greater access to her skin.

He skimmed his hand over her ribs, stroking in a calming manner. He moved to part her thighs, but she had already spread her legs wide in invitation, silently pleading for him to touch her.

His touch ghosted over the smooth folds of her sex, and Sara bit her lip to keep from begging again. He slid one finger along her opening, gathering the moisture pooling along her folds. Sara stared, transfixed, as he brought that same finger to his lips and sucked her essence from the digit before releasing it with an audible pop.

"God, you're sweet." His voice was rough and gravelly.

Sara tossed back her head as he brought his fingers to her pussy again, this time sliding two deep within her core.

SHE WAS LIKE a vise around his fingers, and a cold sweat broke out on his forehead. How the hell was he going to keep from fucking her when she was hot and wet and so damn tight his dick throbbed to be inside her? His wolf snarled at him to mount her, and it was only by sheer force of will that he managed not to slip his skin, shifting right there to take her, staking the claim his animal demanded.

He thrust into her again, and her inner muscles clung to him, seeming reluctant to release him. He rubbed the sensitive flesh on either side of her clit, avoiding direct contact so that he could build her release to something more powerful and hopefully drown out the need that was burning through her like fever in her blood.

Unable to stop himself, he laid a line of kisses down the center of her body, nipping playfully at her navel and making her arch up into him. He took full advantage of her position, cupping her ass and drawing her closer to his mouth.

Jace kissed her pubic mound once, twice, and a third time—gentle, innocent kisses—before he settled himself between her parted thighs and kissed her pussy the way he would her mouth, drawing the plump lips into the heat of his mouth and running his tongue over the hardened tip of her clitoris.

He flicked his tongue, quickly causing her leg muscles to twitch and clench before he thrust his tongue past the spamming muscles of her pussy the way he longed to drive his cock into her. He did it again and again, alternating long, slow licking with fast flicks of just the tip of his tongue and that firm thrust as he fucked her with his tongue until she came, her flavor an explosion that filled his mouth. He knew ingesting her essences would make his own need worse, but he couldn't suppress the need to taste her. He kept his mouth pressed firmly to her flesh as she arched against him as her pleasure crested. Once she'd climaxed, the fever seemed to subside. As her muscles relaxed, she went limp in his arms, and it appeared she was able to rest comfortably.

His own comfort was another story. Pleasuring her had been torture for him, and now that she was snoring softly, his own need for her was burning hot. Jace rose from the bed, careful not to wake her. He went into the bathroom, stripped off his pants, and climbed into the shower, letting icy water pound down his back.

When the cold water failed to wilt his erection, he took himself in hand, jacking himself with hard, sure strokes. Visions of Sara and Caleb intermingled, and he came against the tile of the shower wall, biting his lip against calling out.

It wasn't enough. He was still hard. He still wanted her. Shame that he would think of them both swamped him. He shut off the water. His flesh was cool, but his inner temperature was still raging. Desperate, he began stroking his erection again, squeezing harder than before with a rough violence meant to punish himself for his guilt and lack of control.

He forced the climax from his erection, and still he stayed hard, needing her and missing Caleb—needing them both. He let out a frustrated growl as both man and beast raged at their situation. Jace tried a third round, this time dumping lotion into the palm of his hand. Even though he'd already climaxed, the erection wouldn't go away, and his skin was becoming irritated.

When he came for the third time and still remained iron hard, he wanted to weep. Not knowing what else to do, he forced himself to shift and then change back and to shift again and change back. Agony tore through him with each shift, but the rapid changes had the desired effect. Though he was still semi-erect, his flesh was finally softening. Exhaustion from his rapid changes had sapped his strength, leaving him no choice but to surrender to sleep.

Chapter Seven

The wind was still blowing outside when Sara opened her eyes the next morning. She stretched and snuggled down into the covers before the events of the previous night came crashing back. She'd fully expected Jace to be in the bed next to her and was surprised when she rolled over and found the other side of the bed empty.

She tried to tell herself it was insanity to lust after a virtual stranger as much as she did, but that didn't change how much she wanted him. Even now that desire was building again. Sara hadn't had a lot of lovers. There had only been two in college and one since then. She wasn't a prude or frigid like Nate had accused her of being. It was just that every time she tried to get close to a man, it was as if her body rebelled against the thought. The sex was mundane at best and had even been physically uncomfortable.

It wasn't like that with Jace. She hungered for him with an intensity that scared her, but it hurt that he hadn't taken her last night the way she'd begged him to. She understood why he might have been reluctant. He'd told her he might not be able to stop if she'd changed her mind. Oddly, that thought had been one of the furthest from Sara's mind. She had no doubt he would have stopped if she'd wanted him to. He'd never hurt her. The thought came swiftly, and even though she'd only known him for a short while, she knew it was the truth. She trusted her gut feeling. He might have feared that she was too far gone to make a rational decision, as if she'd been impaired somehow, but the truth was she'd never been so sure of anything in her life.

To add insult to injury, he'd slept on the couch again. It was as if he'd delivered some medical service by giving her pleasure. It was like it was no different than rescuing her from the snow and keeping her from getting hypothermia. Getting her off seemed to be just a task for him that needed to be carried out. Hurt and shame made her feel like a wounded animal, and they were enough to push back the building desire that threatened to pull her under again.

She tossed back the covers, intending to march out to the living room and confront him, but the chill in the air tightened her nipples, reminding her that she was naked. *Maybe you should go to him like this. See if he can hold out for another day.* The wicked thought tempted her to be naughty. It made her want to push his boundaries and see if she could chip away at the wall he'd erected between them.

Sara pulled on the sweater he'd cast aside the night before and threw open the bedroom door. The sight that met her wasn't what she'd expected to find at all, and she fell back a step, stunned.

He was fast asleep—naked, sprawled on the couch, and sporting a huge erection. Sara felt her cheeks heat as she stared at him, unable to look away. She should give him some privacy, maybe cover him up with the blanket that was next to him, for the sake of modesty. Instead she stood gawking at him. She licked her suddenly dry lips and felt as if she were starving and was being forced to look at a buffet laid out in all its glory before her.

Sara clenched her thighs together as she felt her body to respond to the sight of that impressive erection. Her passion tinged only slightly with trepidation.

"If you keep looking at me like that, this hard-on is never going to go away." His voice startled her, and she jumped, her gaze flying to meet his.

Embarrassed to be caught staring, she stammered through an apology and was about to flee back into the bedroom when he bolted up from the couch and captured her hand in his.

"It's a bit late to be so shy, don't you think?" The look he gave her singed her to her toes, and she felt her body respond further to him, readying to accommodate his impressive size.

"This is insane. This isn't normal." Her unexpected reaction to him caused fear to settle in her belly. "I'm not like this. I know women say things like that, but it's true. I'm never like this."

Jace stroked his hand down her arm, and his touch did more to sooth her growing anxiety than words ever could. She moved into his touch, instinctively craving more.

"Sara, we need to talk. I want you so badly, and if we stay in this cabin together, it's only a matter of time before I take you, and we really need to talk about things first."

Her body wept with need at his words, silently begging him to follow through on his promise, even while she gasped, shocked by his blunt statement.

She sighed, and her eyes fluttered shut at the thought that he'd give her exactly what she wanted, but when she opened her eyes, the look he gave her made it obvious that he'd try to hold back, even if it killed them both. "Who's to say I won't take you?" she challenged.

THE IDEA THAT she would challenge him made his wolf restless. It made him want to assert his dominance, and he groaned. He could smell her. She wanted him. She was ready for him, but he couldn't take her. Not until she knew the truth. It was dangerous to tell her what he was. He risked exposure, horrible medical testing, and experiments if she failed to keep his confidence. She'd also have to be told about his relationship with Caleb. If they really were mates, there could be no secrets between them.

He wasn't ashamed of his relationship with Caleb. They'd been lovers for almost two years before Jace left the pack. It wasn't uncommon for males to seek companionship with each other. It had become more commonplace with the shrinking number of females available for mating. He just wasn't sure how to broach the subject.

"Sara, we have no choice but to stay in this cabin. There is nowhere else to go. My truck won't make it out of here, and even if we did, we wouldn't get far," he said, carefully gauging her reaction. If she balked at his words, he'd leave the cabin and shift. He'd spend as much time as a wolf as he could, outside and away from her.

Sara's confusion was evident, and the only thing Jace could think of was comforting her. He came to her, opening his arms, his intent to embrace her clear, and when she stepped into his arm willingly, the wolf inside him wanted to howl in triumph at her show of trust. Though small, it was a beginning, and it spread contentment through him.

She turned her face up to his and kissed him. Her movements were more confident than before, and Jace was lost. All his noble intentions of explaining what he was before he took her evaporated as his passion heated again. Even thoughts of Caleb receded as her tongue tentatively brushed his.

"Talk later. Right now I feel like I'm going crazy." With her words, his control, stretched too thin the night before, snapped, and without further thought to the consequences, he lifted her effortlessly, a rumble of satisfaction escaping his throat when she wrapped her legs around his waist.

The bedroom was only a few steps away, but his cock was throbbing insistently, demanding entrance into the haven he instinctively knew he'd find within her warm, welcoming flesh. Jace feared he'd never make it to the bed. With his wolf riding him hard, Jace had to fight for even a measure of control, but as he placed Sara on the bed and she gazed up at him, trust and acceptance shining in her eyes, he knew he never wanted to hurt her, and suddenly showing restraint didn't seem that difficult.

"You are so beautiful." His words were accompanied by a low rumble in his chest. Sensing his mate had Jace's wolf close to the surface, but being near Sara seemed to calm the wolf enough that the man was in charge, rather than the beast.

Jace slid his hands up the supple skin of her legs. He grasped the hem of her shirt on his way up her body, then whisked it over her head before pausing to take in the sight of her.

HE WAS LOOKING at her like she was a five-course meal, and when his lips descended on her, Sara certainly felt like he would devour her, but as he made contact, she forgot all about being a sacrificial lamb and met his desire head-on.

Jace pinned her hands to the bed, holding them together in one of his, and the gesture made her feel small and feminine. Sara felt his arousal pulse behind the thin fabric of his pants and pressed herself more firmly against him, begging him without words to take her.

Sara dug her nails into his wrist as he continued to tease her. It was a small show of defiance, but it seemed to make the desire in his gaze flare hotter. She arched under him as he drew the rigid peak of her breast into the heat of his mouth, lashing her nipple with the tip of his tongue. He nipped her, and the sting had her gasping. Sara spread her thighs beneath his weight, silently begging for a more intimate touch.

Jace slowly traced the curves of her body, cupping the breast he was devouring before skimming his hand down her center to circle her navel. He followed the movement of his hand with his mouth, and Sara was mindless. Her stomach muscles quivered under the wet caress, and when he sucked the taut flesh of her belly button into his mouth, her pussy clenched in response.

"Please," she begged, unable to bear the empty ache growing within her.

"Soon," Jace answered, his tone comforting.

Sara couldn't keep her hips still when his lips brushed the smooth skin of her pubic mound and he nipped at her labia.

She shivered at the thrill of danger that skittered down her spine.

He released the hold he had on her wrists. He used both hands to make short work of removing his pants, and Sara watched as he sheathed himself in a condom, ignoring the pang of regret she felt at its necessity.

Their gazes met as Jace held her thighs apart, folding them back as he pressed himself into her. Heat flared in her belly as he stretched her, and Sara saw his eyes widen as her unyielding muscles clamped around him as tight as a vise.

JACE CLENCHED HIS jaw, grinding his teeth together with the effort to be gentle. "Mine." The growled claim burst from him when he was fully seated inside her hot flesh, and while he hadn't meant to make the claim, it felt so right, he couldn't regret it.

Jace paused as long as he could, hoping that she would ease around him so that he could move without fear of hurting her. He pulled back, and Sara's flesh clung to his shaft as if it never wanted to part from him.

She wiggled her hips in invitation, and unable to wait any longer, he surged forward again. She groaned and clasped his hips tighter within the cradle of her own, and he was lost. He pushed her harder and faster to her release, enjoying the harsh bite of her nails as she raked his skin.

Jace felt the persistent ache in his jaw that signaled the eruption of his canines and clenched his teeth together, desperate to keep from biting Sara. His cock thickened further within the confines of the condom, and he resented the need for the barrier between them, but until he understood more about what was happening with his intense feelings for Sara, he wouldn't put either of them at further risk.

Chapter Eight

She wanted him again, and the desire frightened her more than she cared to admit, but as she lay in his bed next to him with the sweat of their previous romp drying on her skin, she could already feel need building again.

Sara needed to scratch and claw at him. She wanted to leave her marks on him so that they'd be visible for anyone to see. Sara wondered if it was finding Nate cheating that made her feel so possessive now. She flung an arm over her eyes, trying to block out the burning arousal that was getting hotter and demanding her attention. Sex had never been like this before—she'd always felt detached, as if watching the intimate act happen to someone else without actually feeling it. Now she felt everything and found it confusing to deal with.

She pushed herself up, intending to leave the bed, anxious to be away from him. She was mortified at her reckless behavior, and shame swept through her. Jace growled, low and menacing. It made her jump and had a shiver running down her spine, but she wasn't afraid of him.

"Don't you dare get all caveman on me! I can't believe we just did that! We barely know each other. I need to shower." The note of hysteria in her voice was climbing, and her heart was thumping hard. She wanted his kiss again so badly, she licked her lips in anticipation. "What the hell have you done to me?"

"I wanted to talk, Sara. You told me to talk later." His words were firm but held a hint of regret, as if he should have ignored her and insisted they wait—but he was right that she hadn't wanted to. All she'd thought of was having more, being closer, and forging a connection with him.

"I may have been wrong." She whispered the words as Jace moved to seal their lips together again pulling her back onto the bed and against his body.

"So stop me now." His words were breathed across her lips, but he held back, waiting for her to stop things between them. Instead she closed the minute space between their lips.

His kiss was spicy hot and spread through her like wildfire. She sighed into it, the rightness of their embrace settling into her soul, and he took advantage and deepened the contact, sweeping his tongue inside her mouth to duel with her own.

He'd barely touched her, and she was ready for him again. Ready and begging for him to take her repeatedly. Jace broke the kiss and flipped her to her belly. He licked her, his tongue caressing from the opening of her pussy over the curve of her buttocks before dipping dangerously close to her anal opening.

Sara clenched her butt cheeks together, trying to convey without words that she didn't want his attention there. She felt the sharp sting of his teeth as he bit down on her thigh in retaliation. Her pussy flooded with moisture at his display of dominance.

Sara raised her ass off the bed, presenting herself to him. She whimpered when she heard the foil tearing on a condom packet and sighed when he pressed forward, burying his hard length within her.

Jace thrust forward, and she ground back on him, needing more. Her pussy creamed, making the glide easy as he pumped into her again and again. Sara knew she'd feel every thrust tomorrow, her body battered and tender from the harsh pounding, but still she craved more.

Her hands fisted in the bed covers, and she screamed out as her release swept through her in a violent wave that tore her apart and remade her in the same instant. Finally feeling sated, she snuggled deeper into the covers. She heard Jace moving around as he rose from the bed to dispose of the condom, but she couldn't bring herself to care.

JACE WIPED HER down with the soft damp cloth, smiling when she mumbled in her sleep but failed to acknowledge his attention in any other way. Once she was clean, Jace covered her with the blanket curled around her, intending to get a few more hours of sleep before he got up for breakfast.

Jace buried his face in her neck, enjoying the scent of her hair and skin. Even half-asleep as he was, his tongue came out to lick the pulse point, rasping over it in a slow, methodical caress. He sucked the tender skin of her neck into his mouth, allowing his teeth to graze her. He licked again and froze, his mind instantly alert as the coppery tang of her blood exploded on his tongue.

Jace pulled back, horrified with himself as he watched another drop of her blood well up from the small wound on her neck. He fought the urge to lick that droplet away while he watched it grow and roll down the side of her neck.

Not wanting her to be alarmed when she woke, he took the still damp cloth from the nightstand and cleaned away the evidence of her spilled blood.

It was only a tiny nick. You didn't bite her. It will be fine. Jace tried to convince himself, and for a little while, he actually started to believe his pep talk. Then the flashes started, and he caught snippets of Sara's memories. It was only a tiny bit of her blood that he'd ingested, so it was only the strongest memories he got a peek at.

The pain she'd felt when her grandmother passed away when she was seventeen. The disappointment she had felt when she allowed her college boyfriend to take her virginity. The humiliation she'd experienced when she found her most recent boyfriend with another woman, leaving a hollow ache in her chest that demanded to be filled. The terror she'd felt as her car skidded down the embankment after swerving to avoid the deer that had jumped out in front of her car, and finally the comfort and consuming desire that mingled with confusion every time he touched her.

Sara wanted him in a primal way she didn't understand. It frightened and excited her. She wanted to belong to him even as she feared his possession. He felt her anxiety that he would find her lacking, that he would reject her and leave her and she'd be alone again.

"Oh, baby, no, that's never going to happen." He whispered the words, praying that they would soak into her subconscious, and wrapped his arms around her.

* * * *

Every part of her ached, and Sara wondered if she'd been hit by a freight train. The weight of Jace's arm across her midsection was more than she could manage to move without the risk of waking him, and she began to panic, feeling trapped.

Sara pushed at his arm, not caring if she woke him. She needed to get up out of this bed, out of this cabin, away from him and his potent sex appeal. Jace moved his arm, and she shot out of the bed, forgetting that she was still sore from the accident and now from their marathon of sex.

She ached all over and couldn't hold back the groan that escaped when she moved.

Jace was instantly at her side, seemingly oblivious to the fact that his naked body was on display, concern etched across his features. When he reached for her, Sara wanted to push him away. She wanted to assert her independence, but the need to have him close to her was strong, and it won out as he wrapped his arms around her.

"What the hell did you do to me?" she cried as she laid her head on Jace's chest, comforted by the steady thud of his heart.

"Let me run you a bath. It will help," Jace suggested before lifting her effortlessly in his arms and carrying her into the bathroom. "I should have been more careful. You're still healing from the car accident." He set her on the toilet seat, and Sara had to fight against the urge to cringe. The seat was cold, hard, and unforgiving against her battered flesh.

She was thankful that the tub filled quickly and grateful for the helping hand that Jace automatically offered when she tried to step into the bath. Once she was settled,

Jace left the room, giving her privacy, and Sara found that, though she was happy to have an opportunity to think, she also missed him.

The thought of leaving the cabin now caused an ache in the pit of her stomach, and she was glad that the wind still howled outside. She heard another long, low howl and realized it wasn't the wind at all.

Sara sat up straighter in the bath. All thoughts of relaxation quickly fled as the howl came again, this time seeming closer than the last.

"Jace?" Sara called out to him, seeking reassurance. Her pulse throbbed in her throat as adrenaline flooded her system.

"It's okay, babe. Just enjoy your bath." He didn't sound worried at all, and that did comfort Sara. His casual endearment caused a tingle in her belly. When Nate had called her sweetie or honey or other cute names, she would get annoyed, but having Jace call her babe just made her feel warm and content as a sense of belonging spread through her.

"I'm going to go outside and bring in some more wood," Jace called through the bathroom door moments before the front door banged closed.

* * * *

Jace stepped out onto the porch of the cabin and looked around for his brother. "Ryan! What the hell?" he hissed, his anger clear in his tone. There was no need to yell. Ryan's hearing would be even more sensitive in wolf form then it normally was.

Jace clutched the pants and shirt he'd grabbed from the bedroom and waited for Ryan to show himself. He didn't have to wait long. Ryan came out from behind the line of trees surrounding the cabin, and even though he was Jace's brother, Jace couldn't stop the growl that rose up his throat.

This was why he'd left. His wolf saw another alpha, and he registered the fact that Ryan was an opponent. It didn't matter that Ryan was his older brother. It didn't matter that being away from Ryan and the pack slowly ate something inside of him like acid eating through metal.

Ryan reacted to the sound of Jace's low growl by closing his muzzle and bowing his head, lowering his gaze and flattening his ears against the back of his head. It was a clear message of submission, and it had the desired calming effect on Jace.

"Put these on before Sara finds me talking to a wolf!" Jace snapped, his voice low and annoyed as he tossed the clothes to Ryan and turned to go back inside. Sara was still in the bathroom, and for that he was thankful, but he needed to tell her they had company so she didn't become frightened or come out from the bathroom naked.

Jace didn't think he'd be able to stand another man seeing her naked. His wolf would demand retribution.

"Jace?" Sara called, and he cringed at how his brother seemed to zero in on her so quickly. *Is it something about Sara that makes her more appealing to wolves?* Jace thought that what they were feeling for each other was unique, but maybe it wasn't. Maybe she'd be compatible with another member of his former pack. Maybe she could mate with any wolf.

Jace didn't realize how deeply he was scowling until Ryan spoke from close behind him.

"Easy, brother."

"It's harder to control myself with you here," Jace admitted, hating the shame that filled him. He was an alpha. His wolf was strong, but he should be able to control his wolf in all things. *He* was the ruler, not the beast, but he couldn't seem to control himself where Sara was concerned.

"I'll maintain my distance. I simply wanted to meet this woman who has made an impression on you so quickly, and if the truth be told, I want to see if her behavior is the same as what I witnessed with Hayley. You made me curious when we spoke, and if I'm totally honest, I'm stinging more from Hayley's abandonment than I've been willing to admit."

Jace crossed the room to the bathroom and slipped inside to warn Sara that they weren't alone. She jumped when he entered the room, sending water cascading over the edge of the tub.

"Sara, we have a guest. My brother Ryan is here." Jace handed her a towel from a peg on the back of the bathroom door.

"Your brother?" she asked, accepting the towel.

Jace helped her out of the tub and couldn't keep himself from placing a kiss to the side of her neck. His lips covered the nick he'd made. She groaned, pressing herself against the length of his body.

"He lives close by. He came to make sure everything was okay with the storm."

"Why didn't he come sooner? Why didn't he come when I was hurt?"

"The storm keeps fluctuating. It was worse then, and Ryan doesn't have medical training." Seeing she was still confused, he continued, "Things have also been strained between us recently. He may not have thought to show up before now. Come, let me introduce you." Jace waited for her to dress and then eased open the bathroom door. He was careful to keep his body between Sara and Ryan, his wolf instantly protective of her with another male so close.

THE MAN IN Jace's living room was clearly his brother. They were mirror images of each other, but Sara couldn't help thinking that Jace was the more attractive of the two, and although Ryan hadn't done anything to her, she stayed next to Jace, keeping their bodies in close contact.

"Hello, Sara."

"Hello." Sara reached for Jace's hand as she spoke to his brother, feeling the other man's gaze travel over her. His presence made her nervous. He came forward, and she whined in the back of her throat. Jace stepped in front of her.

"Ryan!"

"I need to know. Please, Jace." Ryan bowed his head slightly, and Jace seemed to relax, but then Ryan moved forward another step, shrinking the distance between them.

"Jace, what's going on?" Sara felt uneasy as Ryan came forward.

"No, enough of this!" The air between the brothers seemed electrically charged.

Sara wrapped her arms around Jace's shoulders and pressed her face into his neck, craving skin-to-skin contact with him.

"I won't hurt her," Ryan said as he reached out to Sara. It was the lightest touch, but it was like he'd burned her. She hadn't wanted him to touch her, but she couldn't explain why. She hadn't trusted her instinct to say no. Instead she had ignored the instinct as it rose inside her. Without thinking or understanding why, she sank her teeth into Jace's neck where it met his shoulder, hard enough to draw his blood. The metallic tang filled her mouth, and the scent of Jace's skin filled her nostrils. Even as she began panicking over her strange behavior, it was oddly calming to be so surrounded by him.

Arousal flared hot and bright, and her flesh started to throb. She didn't care that Ryan was in the room. She didn't care that they weren't alone. She wanted Jace. She wanted him now. Hard and deep within her body, claiming her. She needed Jace to show his brother that she belonged to him so that Ryan would back off. Heat rolled off his skin, and the warmth felt good, calming.

"I'm sorry, but I had to know," Ryan said, stepping away from Sara and his brother.

Once he had put distance between them, Sara was able to think again. The heat building in her receded, cooling to a simmer. She looked at Jace's shoulder, and her hand flew to her mouth in horror at what she'd done to him.

"Oh my God!" The imprint of her teeth was clearly visible in his skin, and blood was slowly welling up in those indents. She could taste his blood, the metallic tang coating her mouth. "I'm so sorry. I didn't mean to hurt you." She turned to leave the room, but Jace caught her hand.

"No. Don't leave. It's okay. You didn't hurt me. It's fine." She knew he was trying to soothe her, but the sight of her bite mark on him was making her hysterical.

"Please let me go. Please, Jace. Please." She let out a sigh of relief when he let her fingers slip through his and she was able to escape back to the bedroom.

* * * *

"You said you'd keep your distance!" Jace snapped the words in his brother's mind using their mental link, his teeth gnashing together to hold back the snarl crawling up his throat.

"I know what I said, brother, but I needed to know. I would never hurt her, but I needed you to let me – "

"Ryan! Why the hell did you have to push things?" Jace cut him off, too upset to maintain their mental link. He shoved his brother against the door, anger filling him. Sara had bitten him. She had drawn his blood, and already he could feel their bond knitting tighter together. She would be harder to resist now.

"Damn it, Ryan! She bit me."

"Calm down, man. I'm sure it will be fine."

"You don't understand. I nicked her this morning, and she bled. It wasn't much, but I was beginning to think it was enough, and now..."

"Fuck!"

"Yeah, fuck."

Ryan cast a nervous glance to the closed bedroom door before his gaze returned to his brother.

"Why didn't you tell me? Why didn't you give me some clue?"

"I didn't know you were going to come in here like that." He could feel Sara's distress climbing even from the other room and wanted to kill his brother for causing this mess.

"Jace, you have to believe me. I would have never taken it that far if I'd known. It's just, the way Hayley was, I had to know if Sara would behave similarly. Hayley couldn't stand to be around me once she'd bonded to the other wolf. It came on so fast, I had to know if it would be the same with Sara."

Jace growled. He couldn't help it. "And are you satisfied now that you've screwed up my life? She doesn't know about us, Ryan. She doesn't know about Caleb. How could you? How could you do something so monumentally stupid? Maybe I should come back and challenge for alpha before you destroy the pack with your rash decisions. Hayley is a wolf. There is no reason they'd behave the same way!"

His brother growled at him, a purely wolf sound emerging from his human throat. "Perhaps you should have explained things to her before initiating a blood bond with her."

His brother's words caused shame to slam into him. He'd wanted to explain things to Sara. He'd even tried, perhaps not hard enough. He'd wanted to tell her everything, but now that he'd shared blood with Sara, he feared that it might be too late to tell her what their bond would mean.

Chapter Nine

Jace needed to run to burn off some of the anger still simmering inside him. He'd managed to calm down slightly once he'd thrown Ryan out of his home, but the emotions he caught wafting from Sara like the most tantalizing aromas had him feeling stir-crazy.

He'd tried to coax her out of the bedroom, but she'd flat-out refused, telling him to leave her alone. Not wanting to test her temper, he'd decided to give in to his wolf and allow him to run free.

He made the change easily, allowing it to flow through him. Once in wolf form, the scents around the cabin became sharper. He could smell the lingering scent of his brother, and it brought the anger he'd felt earlier back to the forefront of his mind. He snorted, shaking his big furry head and turning his gaze back to the cabin, back to Sara. Even with the need to run pressing on him, his desire to stay by her side was nearly undeniable.

He made his way to the river that ran along the east side of the property. It was one of his favorite spots, and he settled down by the edge of the water and laid his head on his paws. He'd been an idiot not to tell her about himself. Now he didn't know how to tell her. Especially since they'd initiated a blood bond. Bonding wasn't required when wolves mated, but it was a deeper, more complete, complex bonding that allowed mates to communicate with each other mentally on their own private wavelength rather than the generic one they used as shifters.

Blood bonding created a need for one's mate and made the touch of another almost unbearable. It wasn't taken lightly because it wasn't something that could be easily undone. So even if Sara rejected their mating, they might always be tied to each other.

It might have dimmed over time if it had only been the small amount of her blood that he had drawn that tied them together, but Sara had bitten him hard and had swallowed blood from the wound, rather than getting just a few drops like he had when he'd nicked her.

He knew he'd have to head back to the cabin to try to explain. He didn't know if memory sharing would be the same for her as it was for his kind when they blood bonded during mating, and he needed to be with her.

* * * *

Sara still felt horrible about biting Jace. She couldn't explain what had come over her when his brother had approached her, but the need to have him away from her was paramount.

Jace had only been gone from the cabin for a short time, but with all the snow, she started worrying that he was outside, exposed to the elements. She tried to sooth herself with the logic that he'd been out collecting wood and other supplies from the shed on his property. He hadn't really been gone that long, but she felt his loss acutely, and if she were honest with herself, she'd begun to see being stranded in the cabin with him as a blessing rather than bothersome. She was even looking forward to spending Christmas with him, though she felt bad that she didn't have anything to give him. She had her camera with her, and she could take some beautiful pictures of nature, but with no way to print the photos, she still wouldn't have a tangible gift for him.

Sara used to sketch before taking up photography, and the idea of drawing for him seemed like it would be something he might enjoy. Without drawing supplies, she'd be limited in what she could produce, but it didn't seem right to spend Christmas with him and not at least give him something.

She was looking for some blank paper on the small desk in the corner of the living room when the door swung open, hitting the wall with a bang. Sara let out a startled yelp, and her hand went to her throat.

"What are you doing?" he asked. "Are you going through my things?"

"I wasn't trying to snoop or anything," she said, surprised at the pain his suspicious tone caused her. She needed to go home. It was frightening how quickly she'd come to depend on Jace. The bond between them was developing too fast. She'd only been with him a few weeks. Maybe if she could manage to get out of here, the crazy feeling rioting through her would settle back to something more normal.

She backed away from the desk, giving up on the idea of drawing for him. The defeat brought with it a definite sense of loss. While she'd been searching for the blank paper, an image had come to her of the wolf from her dreams and a companion. She could see the two clearly in her mind—frolicking in the snow, play fighting.

Excitement had bubbled up inside her until she shook. Sara wanted to capture this new wolf now that she could picture him so clearly. Now, with Jace looking at her like she was a thief skulking around the cabin and violating his things, she wanted to shrink in on herself, sketching long forgotten.

JACE WATCHED HER warily, trying to remember if he'd left anything pack related on his desk. It was unlikely, given that he hadn't officially been part of the pack for several months. He could feel the waves of emotions coming from her as clearly as if they were his own and instantly regretted his outburst. He took a step toward her and cringed when she recoiled from him.

He let out the sigh he was unable to hold back. "I'm sorry, Sara. I'm not used to sharing my space with people. I didn't mean to imply that you were snooping or doing anything wrong." The pain he saw in her eyes faded but didn't disappear completely.

"I was just looking for some blank paper. I wanted to make you a Christmas present."

Her words made him feel like the lowest scum, and he wished he could take back the way he'd snapped at her.

"I'm a jerk, and I'm sorry, Sara." Jace moved toward the desk, opened the lower drawer, and pulled out a stack of blank paper. "Are you okay? I shouldn't have left you alone after what happened with my brother. I didn't anticipate how he'd behave toward you. I didn't expect the way that I reacted to his behavior toward you. It must be very confusing for you. Things have been hectic and intense lately."

Jace wanted to tell her, but he didn't know how to broach the subject. If he told her and it went badly, he didn't know what he'd do. He just had to find the right way to do it. Not knowing how to bring it up, he changed the subject.

"Let's go outside and get some fresh air. You could bring your camera, maybe take some pictures around the cabin." Jace was rewarded with a bright smile, and it made him feel even more conflicted. He had to tell her, and he had to do it soon.

Chapter Ten

Sara saw the wolves clearly in her dreams, and they translated beautifully to paper. She was able to draw several pictures of the two of them together. On a whim, she even drew one where the three of them were together. She'd never been good at drawing people, and she'd always hated drawing herself.

"I'm sorry it's not very Christmaslike in here," Jace apologized. "I don't really want to cut down a tree. The cabin isn't big enough for one, and I hate to waste the wood on something purely decorative, but I'm sure I can bring something in to make it a bit more festive in here."

Sara tucked the pictures she'd wrapped in newsprint on a table beside the couch. It was Christmas Eve, and other than the familiar smells from the kitchen, it wasn't Christmas anywhere else in the cabin. "It doesn't need to be more festive. I've never been much for holidays anyway." If she were honest with herself, the holidays had always been cold and empty. Here in Jace's cabin, away from the real world, she felt warmer and more fulfilled than she ever had before.

If she were honest, she could admit that it didn't matter that she'd only known Jace for a few weeks. She was right where she wanted to stay.

As if reading her thoughts, Jace gestured to the window. "The storm has gotten better. We can probably make it out in my truck now. I get you out of here so you can spend Christmas with your family."

His words were like a blow, and her head snapped back. "You want me to leave?" Her knees knocked together, forcing Sara to sit down on the couch.

"It's not that I want you to leave. It's just that everything has happened between us so quickly. We really don't know each other that well, and while I'm not saying that I don't want to be with you, I just think that we need to slow things down a bit. The weather is finally better. There's no reason to stay trapped in this little bubble together. You must want to get back to your life? Your work?"

Sara dropped her head into her hands, afraid to open up to Jace, but she knew if she didn't tell him how she felt, she'd regret it.

JACE COULD SEE the impact of his words on Sara's face. He could feel the waves of emotions sweeping through her. He wanted to take back what he'd said, but he knew he shouldn't. He should let her go.

He knew what she was going to say. He could feel it before she opened her mouth. Jace went to her, squatting down in front of her to take her hands.

"Please don't make me go. I know it's too soon to feel what I do, but it's real."

Jace placed his finger over her lips to stem the flow of words. He watched tears well in her eyes, and it tore into him.

"It is too soon, but I know what you feel because I feel it too. There are just so many things I need to tell you, things we need to learn about each other."

"Please let me stay. I don't have anyone for Christmas. If you make me leave, I'll be all alone." She spoke from behind his fingers, refusing to stay silent.

Jace moved his hand, only to replace it with his mouth. He kissed her, tasting the tears that left salt crusting on her lips. "Shh. I didn't mean to upset you. You've become very important to me. There's just so much we don't know about each other. Some things I don't know that you'll be okay with."

He could see the wheel turning in her brain as she worked to catch up to his words. The moment she became suspicious and wary was obvious. "I'm not some ax murderer, if that's what you're thinking now. I was in a relationship until about six months ago, though."

Sara physically recoiled at his words. "Do you still love her?"

"My feelings are hard to define. I think a part of me will always love this person, but Sara, it wasn't another woman. My last lover was a man."

SHOCK TORE THROUGH Sara. He'd been in love with another man? Would always love him? Her claws had been ready come out at the thought of him with another woman, and she would have thought that she'd feel the same about the idea of him with another man. Oddly enough, the idea didn't make her jealous. It made her hot. The idea of watching him and his male lover made her burn with excitement rather than jealousy.

"Are things over?" She hated to ask, and she felt like a hypocrite since her own previous relationship hadn't ended that long ago, but she couldn't imagine walking in to find Jace in bed with someone else.

"We haven't been together for a while now, and meeting you further changed things for me, Sara."

"I don't want to go home, then. I'd like to stay here. If you'll have me." Sara hated the way that her voice trembled as she asked. Her lungs burned while she held her breath, waiting for his answer. Jace cupped the back of her neck, fusing their lips together. It was all the answer she needed.

Chapter Eleven

When Sara woke up the next morning, the entire house had been dressed for Christmas. Jace had brought in pine boughs that they laid across the mantle of the fireplace. Red velvet stockings hung in front, overflowing with preserves and candied nuts. The smells from the dinner they were preparing wafted through the air.

Jace had even made a Christmas tree of sorts. He had positioned a potted cedar in the corner of the living room. She'd placed the pictures she'd drawn him around the cedar so that they were there waiting for him to open. She noticed there were also presents wrapped for her in colorful newsprint and tissue.

"Merry Christmas, sweetheart." Jace wrapped his arms around her from behind, enveloping her in a hug that felt like home. "Let's open presents."

Jace led her to the couch and set her present in her lap, urging her to open it. Sara peeled back the paper carefully, one corner at a time, as if it were wrapped in fancy paper rather than newsprint.

Her mouth dropped open when the gift was revealed. It was a hand-carved figure of a wolf and a woman. Her hands were in its fur, stroking lovingly, and a second wolf sat watching.

Sara chuckled. The irony that they had both given each other similar gifts was not lost on her.

JACE TORE OPEN the paper on his gift, and the grin froze on his face when he realized he was staring at himself and Caleb in wolf form. He had his mate, but it was obvious that there was much more to their story, and if she was drawing pictures of Caleb, the "more" involved not just the two of them but Caleb as well.

* * * *

The Christmas festivities passed without much further fanfare. They ate dinner, and Jace hung the pictures that Sara gave him. They now stared out over the living room, and they were stunning. Sara had captured both Caleb and himself in their wolf forms beautifully.

What he couldn't figure out was how. He'd never shifted in front of Sara, and he knew she'd never even seen Caleb, so how she could draw the two of them in minute detail boggled his mind.

"Sara, where did you get the idea for the wolves?" he asked, watching a blush creep across her skin, clearly embarrassed.

"You wouldn't believe me if I told you." Her flush increased.

"Try me. They are breathtaking. So realistic, a little larger than an average wolf." He pushed slightly, wondering if she'd realized that she'd drawn the wolves larger than normal but in perfect proportion. Sara and Jace were cuddled together on the couch, but Jace couldn't take his eyes from the drawings. Seeing Caleb's eyes staring out at him after he hadn't seen him for six months made him ache in a way that he hadn't expected. He'd been truthful when he told Sara things were over between them. After leaving the pack, he hadn't expected to see Caleb ever again.

"I've had dreams about this one." She pointed to picture of him, and Jace became more intrigued.

"For how long?"

"Hmm?"

"How long did you dream about the wolf?"

"A few weeks before we met." She pointed to the other wolf. "This one I didn't see until more recently. They both seemed so real, I had to draw them for you."

Jace stroked a hand down her arm, pulling her closer to him. There was more to the mating bond than he'd ever imagined before. It ran deeper than anyone in his pack had speculated or revealed. Experiencing the bond for himself, he instinctively knew why, having realized how private the bond was.

Everything in him wanted to use his connection to Caleb. He wanted to reach out to him, and it took everything he had in him not to do it. There had to be a reason that she was seeing both him and Caleb in wolf form. Jace just didn't understand what it meant.

SARA FELT CRAZY for admitting to the wolf dreams, but Jace wasn't treating her like she was nuts. It felt good getting the truth out. The dreams had begun feeling like a dirty little secret. She felt guilty and disloyal to Jace dreaming about the other wolf. She didn't understand why she'd dreamed of the big gray animal. When she had the dreams of the black wolf, he often morphed into Jace during the dreams, but she never saw the other wolf as a man. She never clearly saw his face. He was always hazy. Not seeing him was becoming a special kind of torture, and she'd give almost anything to see him, to touch him. She woke up burning in the night for something nameless, and not telling him felt wrong.

* * * *

They were a few days past Christmas. With New Year's looming, there was a ticking clock for Sara to make a decision. She could continue working, taking her pictures, selling them online and writing for another website. She had even sent a few out before Christmas. When she'd asked Jace if she could use his computer, she'd seen the color that stained his cheeks as he no doubt recalled their only disagreement when he'd found her searching his desk for paper to draw with. Jace had given her access to his computer so quickly that Sara had almost laughed at him, but the effort that he was making to put things right between them tugged at her heart, and they'd spent the afternoon going through her pictures as she uploaded them to send off.

Nate's wasn't the only blog out there, but she didn't know how she felt about asking Jace to stay longer.

Her vacation had only been scheduled for a few weeks, and that time was up now. It was time to think about rejoining the real world. She didn't want to broach the subject, though, afraid of what Jace would say, but if she were completely honest with herself, she was beginning to feel like a freeloader and she was starting to miss having access to her things.

In the days since Christmas, Jace had become more distant, and Sara didn't know what to do about it. He was still affectionate. He clearly still wanted her there, but there was an aloofness that hadn't been there before Christmas.

She and Jace talked every night about everything. She'd never felt closer to another human being, and yet the detachment that she felt growing between the two of them was like acid eating a hole in her gut.

* * * *

Jace couldn't justify taking her for himself, not if there was a chance that she was supposed to be Caleb's mate too. It wouldn't be fair to further the mating bond between them without Caleb present. Jace wasn't sure how he knew—he was working on instinct, but he knew that if he furthered their blood bond now, it would throw the balance off if she was supposed to be mated to both of them, and he couldn't risk that her connection to him would be stronger than what she might share with Caleb.

If that was the case, then they needed to be equals. She needed to have them both, to be with them both. He knew that Caleb would love her. And he knew that she would wrap Caleb around her finger.

Jace knew he was thinking about Caleb too hard. The connection between them was fused and rusty, but when he thought about Caleb for too long, it tingled like nerves that had touched a live wire. He knew the moment Caleb opened the connection they shared. Jace tried to shove the door closed again, but it was incredibly difficult.

Images of the two of them together flashed through his mind, torturing him. The gentle touch of Caleb's consciousness soothed as it brushed against his own. It bolstered his resolve not to bond too deeply with Sara, but he would have to reach out to Caleb soon. For now it was too raw and too real. He slammed the connection closed, but it left him feeling empty and alone. Only Sara's scent in the cabin kept his wolf from going crazy.

His wolf wanted to claim. He wanted their mate; he didn't want to wait. Only his sense of loyalty to Caleb held him back. He wasn't sure if Sara would be willing to have a relationship with the both of them, but the first step would be for Caleb and Sara to meet.

* * * *

Caleb felt the probe again. They had been coming more frequently for the past several days. Jace had been under radio silence since leaving the pack. It had shocked them all. Every remaining single female had mourned his loss, even though they had been tested for the mating bond and none of them had been a match.

Things had gone on long enough though. Caleb missed his friend, and with every searing probe of their mental connection, the urge to reach out to him became stronger. With Imbolc, their festival to worship the moon to celebrate the coming spring, on the horizon, it was only right for Jace to be with the pack.

Caleb knew he was staying at his cabin. They had been there several times. Hunting in the area was good, the deer plentiful. The urge to go to Jace and coax him back into the fold of the pack was strong. He knew it would never work—the alpha in Jace was too strong—but in the morning, he intended to go to his friend.

Chapter Twelve

The snow had settled down after Christmas. Jace and Sara spent New Year's Day curled together in front of the fire, but everything was different now. The distance that she'd started to feel brewing between them had split open like a chasm.

"I can head home if you'd like." The offer wasn't as hard to make as she'd thought it would be a couple of weeks ago. More painful were his actions toward her now and the controlled way he behaved. "I know you never intended me to be here this long." It hurt Sara to voice those words.

"Come outside with me, Sara."

The look in his eyes made her insides turn to liquid. It made the hurt melt away. It would be back, but right now she wanted to give him what he wanted. She wanted to be with him.

The air outside was chilly, and Sara shivered and huddled deeper into her jacket. She was bundled in one of Jace's sweaters, and his scent still clung to the collar. It made her feel calmer.

She let out a squeal as Jace tossed her down in a fluffy pile of glittering snow and started making a snow angel.

"I'm sorry, Sara. I know the way I've been has been confusing." Jace pinned her down in the snow, staring down at her. She squirmed as the cold seeped into her jeans, and she quivered at the contrast of heat between them and the cold beneath her.

Sara could no longer hold his gaze. She tore her own away, turning to the line of trees surrounding the property.

"I think we have company." Sara shoved at his chest, suddenly wanting to put distance between them and instantly feeling guilty for being so close to Jace, though she wasn't sure why.

JACE TURNED his head and cursed when he saw Caleb standing at the edge of the woods. He tensed, afraid that Sara might have seen Caleb shift, but Caleb was wearing jeans and a pullover. The shoes he was surprised by. It was difficult to shift and have access to shoes. Unless Caleb hadn't come in wolf form, but Jace doubted it.

He stood and pulled Sara to her feet, careful to keep his body between her and Caleb. He wanted the two of them to meet, but his wolf wasn't ready just yet. The wolf in him wanted to protect her. His wolf wanted to claim her. His wolf might not be able to share.

Jace forced himself to bite back the growl rumbling in his throat as Caleb stepped from the trees and came closer to where he'd been playing with Sara. It embarrassed him to be caught being so carefree with her until he remembered he and Caleb would often horse around the same way. Their games would often end in something more erotic. That thought made the back of his ears heat up.

"Caleb."

"Jace."

The two of them stared at each other for a solid minute before the tension became unbearable. Sara shifted behind him, breaking the spell between them, but Jace couldn't bring himself to let her out from behind him.

Oddly, though, she wasn't acting like she had when his brother came by. When his brother had come to visit, Sara had been content to be shielded by his body. She hadn't wanted the other man to be near her. She hadn't even wanted him to see her, and Jace had felt the same way. This time, she wanted to go around Jace; she didn't want him to block her path. Jace could feel her vibrate against him. He ran his hand down the length of her arm, trying to calm the tremor that ran through her.

"Come inside." Jace was careful to keep a safe distance between Caleb and Sara, and he could see that his caution was making Caleb more inquisitive.

"I wasn't expecting to see you."

"Preparations for the celebration have started. It didn't seem right that you're not there."

THE WOMAN THAT Jace shoved behind him intrigued Caleb right away. He was aware of the tentative bond that strung out between them like a thread, and it was hard to not feel left out, but he could feel her reaching out to him as well. It was difficult to ignore the desire to answer that call.

Jace was trying to hold it together. Caleb could sense his inner wolf and the struggle and strain that maintaining an air of civility was causing his friend. So Caleb tried to be respectful; he tried not to make things harder for Jace.

Her gaze was shining with an intense light, and he felt lost in the honey depths. He made eye contact with Jace, knowing that they needed to talk. Luckily she seemed to sense their need for privacy as well and went into the other room.

"You've mated."

"It would seem so."

Caleb caught sight of the pictures around the fireplace, and his mouth dropped open. "I thought she was human."

"She is," Jace confirmed.

"You've told her about us, then?" Caleb couldn't keep the heat out of his voice. What they were was their biggest secret. It wasn't something that just anyone could be told.

"I haven't told her. Sara doesn't know, but I think that there is more to the mating bond, especially a blood bond, than we ever imagined." Jace nodded toward the pictures, keeping his voice low.

"Then how?" Caleb tilted his head toward the pictures again. "And why is my picture up there with yours?"

This time Jace was the one to eye the door suspiciously, as if Sara would burst in on them at any moment.

"She's had dreams of wolves, of our wolves. Even before she got here. It has to mean something, right?"

"I don't know. Maybe? You're sure she isn't a shifter? Her eyes, the way she responds to you... I think I was starting to feel things through our bond that you kept poking at." Caleb couldn't hold back the growl that rumbled in his throat, and then, thinking of Sara again, he clamped his jaw shut.

"I haven't seen you in six months, and without a word you start prodding at me?" Caleb kept his voice low, though he wanted to yell. "Can we go outside? I feel like we have no privacy." Being indoors close to Jace had his wolf clawing at him.

JACE TAPPED ON the bedroom door, then poked his head inside. Sara was lying on the bed, reading. "Sara, we're going to go get more firewood." There was a look in her eye, as if she knew something deeper was going on, but she only nodded, turning away from him. He let the door close with a quiet click as the latch caught. Jace reached out through their shared bond, trying to sense what she was feeling, but little came through. She had thrown up a wall between them, unconsciously trying to protect herself from getting hurt.

She wasn't stupid. Jace knew that she had suspicious about who Caleb was. He could see them in her eyes, and he could feel her confusion beating at him through the tiny cracks in her wall created by the bond they shared, but he could also sense her trust, and that gave him hope that they would make it through.

The wind had died down outside, but the sun had shifted, and Jace was glad that Sara was now in the cabin. The weather was bitterly cold, and it was only their lycan physiology that helped keep them warm.

Jace made his way toward the woodpile in the yard, casting a look over his shoulder at the house.

"Imbolc is one of our most important holidays, Jace. You need to come home. Please, we all miss you. I miss you." Caleb clapped him on the shoulder, and Jace felt the contact all the way through him.

"I'm not going back, Caleb. I can't. You know I can't."

"I know it drives your wolf crazy to allow someone else to be in charge, but you would get used to it eventually."

It made Jace's wolf growl in defiance. He wouldn't get used to it. He couldn't bow, he wouldn't bend, and he wouldn't hurt his brother or his former pack because his wolf was more in control than the man. It was different for some of them, but Jace had never been able to hold his wolf down.

Caleb held up his hands in surrender, and for a moment Jace envied his ability to back down. He turned his attention to the house again. He couldn't see Sara. He didn't think she was watching, but he knew if he followed the thread of their connection, he'd feel her.

"Can you stay a few days?" Jace knew Caleb had responsibilities in the pack, but he needed the chance to explain things to Sara, and he wanted the opportunity to explore what it might mean to be bonded to the two of them.

Chapter Thirteen

The man had to be Jace's lover. He hadn't introduced him, but there was something in the way they looked at each other. There was a connection there, a deep love that should have made Sara feel jealous but instead just made her wish to be a part of what they felt. If she were honest, part of her ached to be in the center of it.

"Sara, we're back." Jace's voice sounded calmer, and Sara ventured out into the main area of the cabin. "Come meet Caleb."

The desire to be close to Caleb hit her again as soon as she entered the room. She could tell Jace noticed, and she felt guilty about it but was surprised when he urged her toward his friend.

Caleb stuck out his hand to shake hers, and the feeling of an electrical current arched from his hand to her own. She'd had a similar reaction the first time she touched Jace.

Sara pulled her hand back, barely resisting the urge to wipe it against her thigh. Her gaze snapped to Jace, and he smiled reassuringly at her.

"I'm very pleased to meet you, Sara. It's extremely fortunate that Jace stumbled upon you when he did."

Sara cleared her throat, which was suddenly clogged, and tucked her hands in her lap so she wouldn't be tempted to touch Caleb. She wanted to run her hands over the smooth plans of his features. She wanted to cup the hard angle of his jaw in her hand and bury her nose against the hollow in his throat. His darker skin tone reminded her of coffee and rich cream, and she wanted to lick him to see how he would taste on her tongue.

She was embarrassed at her raw reaction to him as arousal began making her ache. His eyes were dark like warm chocolate, but something even darker and more predatory lurked in their depths, flashing back at her. It was the same look that Jace often gave her. Lust filled and hungry.

"Yes, he saved me. I wasn't really dressed for this weather. I should have been paying more attention to the road, but the last thing I expected was for a deer to come leaping in front of my car. But then, I've always been more of a city girl." She confessed to being out of her element and chanced a look in Jace's direction, surprised to find something akin to guilt staining his features. She smiled warmly, hoping to put him at ease.

"Caleb is going to spend a few days here before heading home." Two pairs of eyes watched her carefully, and Sara had to bite back a groan of frustration. She could barely hold back the urge to touch him now. It would be torture to have him here for a few days, but then she remembered that it wasn't a given that she'd be here, that he might want her to leave. She caught her breath, waiting to see if Jace would ask her to go so there was room for Caleb. She held her breath until her chest started to hurt, until Caleb nudged her and she remembered to breathe again.

"That's okay, isn't it?" Caleb looked to her.

"You're asking me? It's Jace's house. You're Jace's—friend." She stumbled over the last. Caleb was more than his friend, and they all knew it.

"If I make you uncomfortable, if you don't want me here, I won't stay."

Did she want him there? It was a loaded question, but remembering the zing of electricity that had shot through her at his touch, it was an easy question to answer. She didn't want him to leave. She nodded, not trusting her voice, her mind a mass of confusion. She looked to Jace to ground her and found him smiling.

"Did you feel it again?"

Sara blushed at his question, remembering how she'd reacted the first time he'd touched her. There had to be something going on with her hormones. She ducked her head, refusing to answer, but that was answer enough.

"It's okay if you did," Jace said, his tone reassuring.

It made her feel a little hysterical, and her heart kicked into overdrive. Her gaze darted from Jace to Caleb. He sat with a relaxed smile on his face, no pressure coming from him.

Sara moved away from both men. Needing space to think, she pressed her back against the window, allowing the cold from the pane of glass to seep into her skin. It helped to clear her mind. She closed her eyes to visually block out both the men and how strangely she was reacting to them.

"You can stay if Jace wants you here, but I can't think of the other stuff right now. I've just gotten used to how quickly things have happened between us, Jace. I can't focus on anything else."

CALEB WATCHED SARA leave the room, his hand still tingling from their contact. Jace shot him a meaningful look. They communicated without words, and Caleb nodded. Sara was undoubtedly his mate. Wolves could choose who they mated with—most shifters had that luxury—but finding your bonded mate was different. It didn't happen for everyone. It was like finding your soul mate. They were the one true being you were meant to be with. There was also no denying that she was Jace's bonded mate. It was rare for a human to mate with a shifter and unheard for one to bond with two of them, but it was unmistakable.

"What does it mean?"

"I don't know, but you did feel it, didn't you? The connection, the awareness that she's your mate too. I'm not crazy. It was there for you too, wasn't it?"

Caleb nodded. "Yeah, I felt it, and I'm pretty sure she did too. I just don't know what to do about it."

"Give her a bit of time. Just give her a chance to come around. If it happens like it did with us, things will happen quickly. It was like lightning. I imagine it will be the same for your wolf now that he's aware of her."

"I can't believe you found her."

Jace had told him about the accident when they were outside. He'd been totally honest about how he'd been hunting the deer and caused her accident.

Caleb shuddered, thinking about what would have happened to her if Jace hadn't found her in time. Jace was right—now that he was aware of her, all he wanted to do was go into the room she'd retreated into so that he could be with her. He'd smelled her arousal as it built. She wanted him but was swamped with confusion.

"Has she told you about the dreams? Are they just of the wolves, or have they been about us as well?"

"She's embarrassed by the dreams. She doesn't understand them, so she hasn't said much about them. I'm not sure what they mean, but they could be connected to why she can be a mate to our kind. Or it could be a symptom of our bonding."

"I've never heard of wolves sharing a mate. Maybe it's because she's human?" Caleb asked.

"Maybe. I don't know. I've never heard of a human mating with a wolf before."

Caleb glanced toward the other room, assuring himself that they were still alone. "Should we consult the council?"

Jace growled at Caleb's suggestion.

* * * *

That night her dreams were filled with both of them. She tossed and turned, swamped with erotic thoughts of the two of them touching her, holding her. She thrashed as they caressed her, making her moan and arch toward them, pushing into rather than pulling away from hands that trapped her, pressing her to the mattress. She whimpered as they whispered all the naughty things they wanted to do to her.

She jolted awake, crying out for them. She was alone for only a moment, panting in the darkness, before Jace was there, his weight dipping the bed.

"Hey, shhh. Are you okay?" She shifted toward him, wanting to be closer, but it wasn't enough. She needed something else—someone else.

"Caleb," she whined, and the bed dipped on the other side of her.

"I know this is hard, sweetheart." Caleb's voice whispered across her skin.

She arched again, renewed visions from her dream swamping her. "Please, I need—"

"Shh, it's okay. Everything is going to be okay," Caleb soothed.

Caleb and Jace kept enough space between their bodies so they weren't touching her. "Just breathe through it. It will pass."

"It hurts!"

"I know. I know, but it's going to be all right," Jace said, keeping his voice soft.

"It's like before, Jace. Not as bad, but it still hurts." She twisted on the bed, trying to find some semblance of relief. She writhed as another wave of pain hit her. "Oh, please make it stop."

"Come on. Let's get you up and into the shower. It might help."

She reached for Jace as he lifted her and carried her into the bathroom. He propped her up against the sink while Caleb ran water in the shower.

Her gaze shot to Caleb's when Jace moved to raise the nightgown she was wearing. A small sound of distress gurgled up her throat.

"I'll go," Caleb offered.

Jace gave a slight nod, but Sara flung out her arm to rest a hand on his shoulder. "No, please don't." She let Jace raise the nightgown and arrange her under the spray of water.

Sara sighed as the water caressed her sensitized skin. Caleb had set the water temperature to just above lukewarm, and it felt wonderful on her heated flesh. It was enough to cool the arousal so she could think.

"What the hell is the matter with me?" She hated the way her voice shook with panic.

"Nothing's wrong with you, sweetheart. Nothing at all. It's natural."

"It's not!" she wailed, clutching tighter at Caleb's shoulder.

Sara let her head hang forward. It didn't feel normal. It felt crazy. She wanted them both, and despite spending time with Jace, she still felt like she should know him better. None of it mattered as she pressed herself harder against Caleb, enjoying the play of solid muscle against her softer flesh.

If Jace had been angry or had shown any sign of disapproval, she would have pulled away, but he didn't. He groaned and smiled at her, stepping back to give her and Caleb more space. It was the only encouragement she needed. Her body knew what she craved, and she wasn't beyond taking it.

She needed him to touch her. It had helped the first night this reaction had happened with Jace, but then it progressed beyond touching. She'd needed Jace deep within her, quenching a thirst she'd never experienced before.

Now it was Caleb's touch that ran over her flesh, calming the persistent throb. He cupped her breasts, thumbing her nipples. She pushed their weight into his hands, impressively large hands that held her though she still managed fill his palms to overflowing. She wanted him to take her, but he held back.

"Not yet, Sara. Not yet."

She begged, but he still refused to give in to her.

Chapter Fourteen

After the water had pounded down on them for a while, she was much more levelheaded. She still wanted them both, but she felt more rational about it, more in control. They needed to talk about how things would be.

"So have the two of you done this before?"

"This?" Jace asked.

"This." Sara gestured between the two of them and then to herself. "Shared, shared a woman—a lover?" She felt a twinge of jealousy as she considered the idea.

"No. Never."

She let out the breath she'd been holding. "But the two of you have—" She stalled. "Together, I mean." She knew they had, but she needed it confirmed.

Caleb laughed. "Have we had sex? Are we lovers? Yes, Sara, we have."

"Then what do you need me for?" There was hurt in her voice. It colored her tone, but she couldn't keep it from bleeding in. Her recent experience with Nate had left her feeling raw.

"We need you." From Caleb.

"We want you." From Jace, and they both reached for her in that moment. "You feel it too, don't you?"

She nodded, unable to deny their claims. "I thought you weren't together anymore." She hated the way her voice shook as she sought answers from Jace.

"We weren't, Sara. I didn't lie about that. I hadn't seen Caleb for almost six months."

"You want to be together again though." She made it a statement.

"Yes, but with you," Caleb said, and his blunt words made heat race into her cheeks. Again she looked to Jace for confirmation.

His gaze never wavered from hers as he nodded. "There has to be balance in this though. That's why it has to be the two of you. At least at first. We've already been together. We've been together alone. The two of you need that."

Sara had been on board with having sex with Caleb—she'd even been willing to have sex with them both together, and she could even imagine the two of them having sex—but what she couldn't fathom was having sex alone with Caleb right now.

"No." She clutched Jace's arm, refusing to let go.

"No?"

She shook her head at Jace's question. "No, not without you here." It felt wrong to be with Caleb without Jace there. She clung to him harder, unwilling to loosen her grip in case he was adamant that she be with Caleb alone and forced the issue by walking away.

"It's okay, Jace. It's okay," Caleb said, and Sara wasn't sure if he was trying to soothe her or reassure Jace.

The two of them shared a look that Sara couldn't decipher.

"There's always an alpha, Jace. It's all right. Really, there's no need to cause Sara distress."

JACE SEARCHED CALEB'S gaze for some sign that he was really okay. Jace knew that if he stayed with them this first time, his bond with Sara would likely be stronger than her bond with Caleb.

Caleb nodded again. It was then that Jace saw it. Caleb wanted this. He wanted it exactly like this. It was perfect, but Jace didn't know how to begin. He'd never done this before. They'd never done this *together* before. He knew what he would do with Sara if they were alone. He knew how he'd begin with Caleb, as he had countless times before.

As if sensing his turmoil, Caleb moved forward and kissed Sara, a consuming kiss that took possession of not only her lips but of her as well, and when he was done kissing her, he turned his attention to Jace, reaching for him.

Jace leaned forward, and their lips met over Sara's head. It was a soft touch at first. A delicate meeting that quickly became more as Caleb licked the bow of Jace's upper lip, and through the layers of the kiss Jace became aware of the scent of Sara's arousal growing stronger, even through the veil of the water around them. She was clearly turned on by the sight of them together.

Caleb's fingers dug into his neck, and Sara whimpered as if she felt the bite in her own skin. Needing to do more, Jace took control of their movements, tearing his mouth from Caleb's to bury his lips against Sara's throat. He licked the throbbing pulse at the base of her throat.

His desire to bite her was strong, but they wouldn't mate her, not yet. They wouldn't even both take her yet. He should have told her what he was before they'd slept together, and he hadn't. It wasn't something that he felt good about, but his loyalty needed to be to the safety of his people first.

He nodded to Caleb, who ran his tongue along the other side of her throat. This would be how they mated her. They would both bite her as they came inside her. Sara would feel the need to bite them as well, and while she wouldn't crave the blood as his kind did, her bite would link them all together.

Jace reached around them both and shut off the water. It seemed to spur Caleb into action. Jace watched as Caleb pulled down his boxers. He licked his lips, watching as Caleb lifted her out of the shower and carried her back to the bedroom.

HER DAMP SKIN stuck to his own like they were already fusing together. He could sense Jace's gaze on them, and it made his heart thump harder. Jace was his alpha. The other politics of the pack didn't matter, and this was their woman. The suffering that Caleb had gone through in the last six months would all be worth it now.

The ridicule he'd endured and the danger he'd put himself in when members of his pack found out where he was going. Jace had isolated himself from the pack, and although the pack wanted him back, his desertion was still a betrayal. If the pack learned that Caleb was going to find Jace and that he intended to bring him back with him, it was possible they would view him as a traitor. The way Jace watched them now, with a look of ownership in his eyes, made it all worthwhile.

Caleb laid her out on the bed, knowing just how Jace wanted things to play out, their once silent line of communication now very active. It might have put Sara at a disadvantage that they could decide how to proceed without her knowing, but once they mated, a path of communication would be opened, and she'd share something similar with Caleb could already feel himself preparing for her presence.

He placed her on her hands and knees, her ass on display, and he felt the shiver of awareness that shuddered through her as she realized this.

"Shh, it's okay, baby. Let us make you feel good." She calmed instantly, though whether it was his words or the comfort she received from Jace, Caleb didn't know.

She was wet and ready for his entry, but he hesitated, wanting to prolong the moment. Unable to resist, he ran his hand over her flank and followed the moment with a line of kisses. He accepted the condom that Jace handed him. Lycans were immune to disease, but with her being human, he didn't know if pregnancy would be an issue, and he sensed Sara would be more at ease, needing to remind himself that they were still strangers to one another despite the connection already flourishing between them.

He took his time entering her. This time there would be little foreplay, but she was aroused to the point that he slid in easily. Once fully seated, he paused to allow her to adjust to his girth. Then she rocked toward him, and he withdrew and thrust forward again. She grunted, and her walls contracted on him.

The bed dipped. Caleb looked up to find Jace with one knee on the edge of the bed as he fed Sara his cock. She moaned, an erotic, muffled sound around his flesh, and Caleb watched as Jace's erection disappeared between her lips.

They timed their moments to work in tandem, learning the rhythms that they would need when they took her together. Caleb praised her, and Jace whispered dirty things in her ear. He knew the types of things that Jace was saying because he'd been on the receiving end of those comments numerous times. Her muscles clamped down on him, and she screamed around Jace, pulling back as she climaxed so hard that she gritted her teeth.

* * * *

Sara was sandwiched between them, sleeping peacefully, and Caleb could easily picture many nights this way. He didn't want to wake her, but he was restless and needed to run. He met Jace's gaze over her shoulder, and Jace nodded. They both slid out of the bed, tucking the blankets around Sara so she'd remain warm.

The snow was coming down hard again, and rather than move into the woods to shift, Caleb and Jace stripped off their clothes on the porch and changed quickly to their wolf forms.

"I had no idea that it would be like that." Caleb used their mental connection to communicate.

"We need to find a way to tell her. We have a hard road ahead. I don't know how the council is going to react."

Caleb growled and tossed his head. The council would likely rip her apart. Humans didn't know about their kind. Their interactions were minimal, and two alphas mating a human would be a huge scandal. The only saving grace was the fact that shifters couldn't control who they mated. The council would have to take that into consideration.

Jace nipped at him, urging him toward the river that ran along the southern edge of the property. They chased each other across the pristine blanket of snow, playing like no time had passed. They pursued each other in turn, oblivious to the fact that hours had passed.

"We should get back to the cabin before Sara gets up." Jace made the suggestion, already turning to back in the direction of the house.

JACE RACED FORWARD, his strong legs eating up the distance quickly. The journey was still nearly half an hour, and he cringed, not having realized before how far from away from the cabin they were, never intending to leave Sara alone and unprotected for so long.

When he reached the line of trees that surrounded the property, he skidded to a halt, the scent of an unfamiliar shifter hanging in the air and making the hair on his haunches stand up.

He scented the air, looking for any sign that Sara was in danger. He let the change slide through him, concern for Sara making him blind to everything else. He was already back in his human form when he heard the sound of a glass shattering and a surprised gasp.

Caleb was still in wolf form behind him. Jace hung his head in embarrassment. His vision had been so clouded with thoughts of Sara's safety that he hadn't seen her sitting on the swing in the corner of the porch.

"Shit!"

"What? How? What?" Her voice sputtered.

"It's okay." He stepped forward, his hands held out in front of him. He stopped when Sara shrank back from him. "Damn it!" He cursed again but kept his distance. "I won't hurt you. Let me come get my clothes. The cold was starting to seep into him, and he shivered. Though he suspected it was fear of Sara's reaction that really made him shake. Jace stepped onto the porch, careful to keep enough space between him and Sara so that she might feel safe.

"Check out the scent," he urged Caleb using their mental link. He needed to explain to Sara, but he also needed to know who'd been poking around. When she didn't balk or retreat again, he went into the house.

"When I saw your clothes on the porch, I thought—I don't know, I thought the two of you had gone off alone. That I wasn't enough for you, that you didn't want me." Sara sank down on the couch, watching as Jace pulled on a pair of sweatpants.

"I want you, Sara. Never doubt that."

"Just not enough to tell me the truth." Jace hated the hurt that lingered in her tone. Her eyes flashed with anger when Caleb walked through the door.

"We couldn't tell you. I wanted to—we both wanted to—but we couldn't." Jace watched as she shuddered, trying to pull together her composure.

* * * *

"I've been here for weeks. In your bed for weeks. You've been inside me, and in all that time you couldn't think to say, 'Sara, I need you to know I'm not human.' Jesus! Was anything we shared real, or am I just that big of a fool?"

She sat on the sofa, watching him pace back and forth like a caged animal, and gave a snort of laughter when she realized how accurate of a description that was.

She was surprised to find she wasn't mad at him. Not for being a wolf anyway, but she was angry that he hadn't told her. It had been shocking to see him emerge from the large creature that had charged into the yard, but even in shock she recognized him. She'd been dreaming of him long before coming to the cabin.

Sara could vaguely recall regaining consciousness in the snow with him staring down at her. All the erotic dreams she'd had about the wolf came rushing back to her in a hot tide. Somehow she'd known it. Her subconscious had been trying to tell her what he'd refused to.

"Sara, please try to understand. What we are is a huge secret. It's not something we share with just anyone."

His words felt like a kick to her midsection. "I didn't think I was just anyone." She couldn't meet his gaze when she made the statement. It simply hurt too much. She'd begun to believe that they were more to each other, that they could have more together. Suddenly her crazy reaction to them both began to make sense. "I need to go."

"Please don't leave," Caleb chimed in. "We can work this out." He came forward and squatted down in front of Sara, bracing his forearms on her knees.

"No, no. I have to go today. Now. Right now." She pushed his arms from her legs and jumped up, determined to grab her things.

Chapter Fifteen

By the time her things were thrown back into her suitcase, the shock had worn off and fear had finally set in. The man she'd been sleeping with was a wolf, wasn't human. How was she supposed to come to terms with that?

She didn't know how to and was desperate to return to something normal. The desperation made her scramble to leave, and she'd made Jace drive her into town. He'd offered to drive her all the way home, but she couldn't imagine being stuck in a truck with him for the hours that it would take to get there.

"I know you need some time. We understand that, and I know it's not fair to press the issue, but I need you to promise that you won't tell anyone about us."

Sara laughed. It was a bitter sound filled with very little humor. "Who would believe me if I did say anything? People will think I'm crazy."

"Sara, come on. It isn't as bad as all that."

"Not as bad? Not as bad? You're not human! You're, you're, I don't even know exactly what you are, but what I do know is that you lied to me. I'll keep your secret. I won't tell anyone, but that's it. I'm done."

"Please be careful. There were other wolves around the house. That's what made me shift in the first place. I don't know who they were or why they were there, and I need you to be cautious. You can't just leave and have that be the end of it."

"God, this is so messed up!"

"Please, Sara. I wouldn't ask you for this if it wasn't important."

"Fine. I'll keep your secret. I'll stay in contact. We'll talk about things later, but right now I just need to go home."

* * * *

Now that she was home, she wanted to be back in the cabin. The house was stale from being shut for several weeks. Sara opened the drapes and the windows, letting fresh air clear out the lingering dust motes. It was obvious Nate had been staying somewhere else while she'd been gone. Likely staying with the woman she'd found him in bed with.

There were half a dozen messages on her machine from him, apologizing again for his behavior and telling her he wanted her to come home, then a pile of angry messages where he demanded access to his stuff. Sara wondered where he'd ended up staying if it hadn't been with his new lover and why he hadn't bothered to just get his stuff while she was gone, but her curiosity wasn't strong enough for her to pick up the phone and call him. Probably because he wanted to be sure she was home. He always had preferred a big scene, she thought with a snort, skipping over his last message. She played the other dozen calls from a few of her friends wondering where she'd gone and why she was AWOL.

Sara returned several calls, refusing a couple of invitations to go out for dinner or drinks. Instead she went online to search for magazines and blogs hiring freelance photographers. The magazine that Nate worked for had asked her to continue working with them shortly after Christmas, but Sara had refused. Since the magazine belonged to Nate's best friend, it was only a matter of time before she'd have to see or hear about Nate, and she wanted nothing to do with him.

Once fresh air was circulating through the house, Sara felt better, but the rumpled sheets on the bed soured her mood. She stripped the sheets with short, jerky, angry movements and threw them in the garbage, cursing Nate for the loss of her favorite sheets.

She was cursing Jace and Caleb and men in general when she was grabbed from behind. Sara kicked back at the person holding her and bit into the meaty flesh of the palm covering her mouth, but they held fast.

Sara bit down harder, tasting blood, but she couldn't break herself loose. The man holding her shook her hard, hitting her in the side of the head in an attempt to get her to let go. Sara's head snapped back, and she bit down on her own tongue.

"The stupid bitch bit me!"

"Did you really expect her to be a kitten and come with you easily? Come on. Quit fucking around. Let's get the hell out of here before someone sees us."

Sara spit the blood from her mouth and tried to scream, but before she could make a decent sound, she felt the sharp jab of a needle in her neck, and blackness claimed her.

* * * *

Sara wasn't sure how much time had passed when she came to, and she had no way of knowing where she was. The only thing that she was certain of was that her mouth felt like cotton and her head throbbed. She groaned, gingerly touching the area where they'd stuck her with the needle, and briefly wished that she'd kicked her attacker in the balls.

Her face felt hot and swollen where he'd struck her, but after taking inventory of her injuries, she figured that she was okay. She just had to remain calm and use her brain.

"You're awake."

Sara flinched, not having realized that she wasn't alone in the room. She clamped her lips together, refusing to make a sound, not wanting to give her captors the satisfaction.

"Oh, come now. Don't be like that." The man chuckled. Sara wasn't sure if he was one of the same men who had broken into her house.

"What do you want?" Her voice cracked. The man leaned forward, offering her a glass of water, which she was reluctant to take. They'd already drugged her once. There was no way she'd accept food or drink from them.

"Sara—it is Sara, right?" He went on without waiting for her to answer. "You know something you're not supposed to." He wagged his finger at her, as if scolding a child. "They broke our biggest, most important law when they showed you what they were."

"I don't know what you're talking about." Her voice broke again, feeling like it was pulled roughly from her throat. Her captor shoved the water at her again, gripping her by the throat when she refused his offer. She thrashed, tossing her head as the tepid water spilled over her lips.

"Stop being so stubborn. I don't want to hurt you."

Sara coughed as she swallowed the water wrong. Her captor hauled her up and thumped her on the back. Tears leaked from the corners of her eyes as she struggled to draw breath into her lungs.

"They really shouldn't have dragged you into our world, but now that they have, I intend to find out what makes you so special. The Coldridge Pack has always been at the top of the food chain. Favored by the council, given all the perks. Well, no more. There is something about you, and it's the key to figuring out our mate issues. Then the Yellow-Claw Pack will be the ones who'll curry favor with the council and get all the perks."

* * * *

Sara's mind was reeling. Alone in the dark, she kept thinking about the packs her jailor had mentioned. She didn't know what the hell he was talking about. She didn't understand pack politics; she didn't even know how many packs there were. She's been thrown into a world she didn't understand, and Jace had been so busy protecting the secret of his genetics that he hadn't prepared her for anything like this. Lying on the hard, lumpy mattress in a room without windows, Sara had no idea how long had passed since they took her. She had tried to keep track of the time by keeping track of when they fed her, but the meals were all the same, and she had no way to know if she was eating breakfast or dinner. She'd eaten several times, which either meant they were overfeeding her to make her think she'd been here longer than she had or that they'd held her for at least three or four days.

The only people she'd seen were the man from the first day and the man she'd bitten the day she was taken. So far they hadn't really hurt her. They'd questioned her about her relationship with Jace, and she thought they'd meant to hit her when she refused to respond. They had asked her a thousand questions about her past and her life, but there was nothing she could think of and nothing she was willing to share.

The next time the man came into the room, he was carrying a tray covered with cloth, a cold, hard look on his face, and Sara shuddered.

"Today we're going to try something different. You've been so quiet, Sara, so unwilling to cooperate, so today we're going to see what your blood can tell us."

He lifted the cloth to reveal a lethal-looking syringe, and a scream welled up in her throat. Sara's fight-or-flight response kicked in, and she bolted from the bed, running for the door he'd left partially open. She made it to the entrance before he yanked her back.

"No!" Sara clung to the door frame, kicking back with her feet. Her captor grunted when she made contact but didn't loosen his grip on her. He tossed Sara back on the bed and slammed the door behind him.

"We haven't tied you up. We haven't mistreated you—much. Don't make us change that." He held her down.

Sara whimpered as the needle slid into her arm. He took several vials of her blood, leaving Sara feeling woozy with the room spinning wildly.

Chapter Sixteen

Jace had a bad feeling as soon as he dropped Sara off. He trusted her to keep his secret. He knew he was stupid for keeping the secret from her in the first place, and the sense that she wouldn't call grew like a lead ball in his stomach.

She didn't call the first day. He'd expected it, but it still made his skin crawl with unease. He started imagining what he would go through if she renounced his mate claim.

Mating was a deep bond, a marriage between shifters, and it was a bond that was rarely broken. It could be done. He could set her free, but it would take months of being apart, and they'd go through withdrawal-like symptoms. It would be difficult, but he'd let her go, and eventually they would both be able to go on with their lives.

He called her the second day, and the hair stood up on the back of his neck when she didn't answer. The feeling only grew stronger when she didn't answer again.

"Caleb, something isn't right. I'm going to her house."

"I thought she had you drop her off in town."

"She did, but I convinced her to give me her phone number and address before she got out of the car. Now she's not answering, and it isn't right." Jace tried to ignore it, but he couldn't.

"Don't you think that maybe you're overreacting a bit?"

"You said yourself that you thought the scent on the property was Yellow-Claw. What if they were here to hurt her?"

Jace tried to trace the mental pathway that had begun between them but couldn't pick anything up. "It's been three days now, and we haven't heard a word. I'm going."

* * * *

Caleb came with him, refusing to allow Jace to walk into an ambush or to leave Sara to fend for herself. What they found when they entered Sara's house made Jace wish he'd followed her home. He wished he'd never allowed her to leave in the first place. The scent of her blood lingered in the air, and it had his wolf raking at his ribs as his anger rose. The room stank of her fear and the now familiar scent of the wolves that had been on the property.

It was clear they had taken her and obvious from the presence of her blood that they had hurt her. "Damn it! I knew something was wrong!" Jace reached out to her, trying to sense her. There was a hot flash of pain, then dizziness, and then nothing.

Leaving the house, Jace carefully followed the scent as far as he could, but having been three days, the trail quickly went cold.

"Shit!"

"What will we do now?"

"We're going to have to go to the council. If we approach the Yellow-Claw Pack, it could start a war with them. We'll have to get the council's approval first."

* * * *

They took more blood, and Sara started to worry that eventually they would take too much. She had no idea what they were doing with her blood, but it couldn't be good. She began to suspect they might never let her go.

She regretted having left Jace and Caleb. It had been fear that kept her from staying with them, but now, having the time to reflect, she realized that she'd never felt safer than she had with them. She wanted more time with them.

The room was always dim, with no natural light and only a single bare bulb. It began to impact her mood, and only thoughts of the two of them kept her from losing all hope.

Her dreams were more vivid than ever, featuring both Jace and Caleb. In her dreams, she was always at their mercy, caught between them as they pleasured her. She was careful to keep her reactions hidden from her captors, afraid that if they knew the true depth of her desire for the two wolves, they would devise more ways to torture her.

"No, no more," she said as the door swung open and her captor appeared with the now familiar tray. "No more blood. No more needles. No more!" Her arms were covered in bruises where they had taken blood samples from her. "What are you trying to do? You need to let me go." Her voice broke as she sobbed out the last, more a plea than the demand she'd meant it to be.

* * * *

"What the hell do you mean you know the Yellow-Claw Pack has her?" Jace felt his wolf clamor to break free as he took in the smug faces of the nine council members. He knew attacking them would be a death sentence, but that didn't stop him from wanting to do it anyway.

"Darius came to us with some very disturbing news about how you were on the cusp of mating with a human. He suggested that there might be something about her that's allowed her to be compatible with you. We oversee all the packs, not just the Coldridge Pack. We can't be seen to show favoritism."

Jace lunged forward, and it was only Caleb's hand on his shoulder that managed to restrain him.

"Calm. We don't stand a chance of saving her if they kill you."

Jace reined in his temper, but just barely.

"She's human."

"Yes, and as such she shouldn't have had any dealings with the two of you, but when Darius suggested that she may hold answers or even the cure to our fertility issues, we couldn't let the opportunity pass to put his theory to the test."

"Have they hurt her?" Caleb asked, and Jace felt bile rise in his throat.

"Simple, relatively noninvasive tests. They had originally wondered if she might be compatible with one of them as a mate, but she seemed repulsed by the touch of other males." The elder narrowed his gaze on both of them, as if they'd done something wrong.

This time the growl that sounded belonged to Caleb. "You allowed them to touch her. You sanctioned the rape of an innocent woman, a human who knows next to nothing about us or our ways?"

Leo, the oldest council member, partially shifted so that only his hand was that of a wolf. It was a rare ability among shifters and normally came with advanced age and power. He lashed out and grabbed Caleb by the throat, squeezing until the razor-sharp points of his claws drew blood and the blood soaked into the collar of Caleb's white T-shirt. Leo growled.

"We are the council. We rule. Your role is not to question what we know to be right. One such as you, who would have mated another male from your pack, depriving your pack of powerful offspring, that you would dare dilute our great lineage with that of a human." He spat the words in disgust before he released Caleb, flinging him away from him. "Do not question your elders, pup."

Caleb's hand went to his throat, and he coughed violently.

Seeing his lover on the floor, his chest heaving as he fought to breathe, and not knowing where Sara was, Jace decided to try another strategy. Jace sank to his knees, prostrating himself in front of the council. They were pompous old bastards who needed to be removed from their base of power, but if begging them was the only way to ensure Sara's safety and to stop further attacks on Caleb, he would put his pride aside to protect them both.

Jace let his head hang low, cocked to one side so his throat was exposed. "Please. We need her. Please don't allow her to be hurt anymore."

"It was foolish of you to become involved with a human," Leo snapped, gnashing sharper-than-human teeth at Jace, flaunting his power. Jace felt his own power rise in answer. He ground his teeth together as his own incisors and claws grew in retaliation to the challenge Leo was throwing down.

Jace had been able to partially shift from an early age, almost as soon as he'd been able to shift. It was a skill that young wolves rarely possessed and showed the immense power of his inner animal. It was a power he hadn't shown the council. They would have seen him as a threat to their power base, and there was no telling what they would have done to eliminate that threat. As young as he'd been then, it was unlikely that he would have been able to defend himself against them. Now he had little doubt that he could not only defend himself but defend his mate as well, and he would have loved nothing more than to tear out the throat of the nine men sitting in front of him for what they had allowed to happen to her.

Instead he knelt lower and ripped the collar of his shirt further, exposing bare flesh while he repeated his plea for Sara to be saved. "The bond has already partially begun with us. She won't mate with another."

"You can't presume to know that," Leo snapped, and Jace wondered if the others would speak at all or if they were truly one unit. He hated the taunting look that Leo gave him and wondered if they had really tried to forcibly mate Sara to others or if everything Leo said was some type of game for his own amusement.

Jace raised his eyes just long enough to make contact with Leo's gaze. "I do know, because that woman is my mate. She is *our* mate. Please, you must give her back to us."

A heavy wooden door behind them was thrown open, and Jace's head snapped up when the scent of her hit him. Sara was shoved through the door and fell to her knees. Jace was on his feet and at her side before he could contemplate any possible repercussions. Darius sneered at him from the door, and Sara cowered at the sound of the man's snarl. The scent of her terror grew as Darius growled. She whimpered, and the sound made the other man's lips curl maliciously.

"Shhh. It's going to be okay. We'll get you out of here."

Hearing his words, Leo thumped a hand down on the table. "You haven't been dismissed, pup." He spat the insult at Jace, and a wave of power slammed into Jace.

It was difficult to restrain his own wolf. The sight of Sara shaking helped him maintain control. She looked like she was barely holding herself together, and Jace feared traumatizing her further.

"We will keep the samples she provided to help us find a solution to our fertility issues. We will monitor the mating, and you will rejoin the pack."

Caleb gasped, and Jace recoiled as if he'd been physically struck.

Leo went on. "If you fail to comply, there will be consequences for the woman."

Leo's meaning was clear. If they didn't do what the council wanted, the council would kill Sara. No human could know about lycans. It was far too risky for their race as a whole.

Anxious to take Sara away from the horror she'd been through, he bowed his head, agreeing to their decree.

Chapter Seventeen

Leo had barely given him permission to move before Jace had Sara scooped up into his arms and he and Caleb were striding toward the door. Jace knew he wouldn't have much time before the pack came calling for him. He'd be expected to resume his position in the pack, and if he couldn't subdue his instincts, he'd be forced to fight and kill his own twin brother.

The thought had his muscles tensing, and Sara whimpered as he squeezed her too tightly. The bruising that was on her body was extensive where they had drawn her blood. It was obvious they'd been rough with her, even if they'd intended otherwise, and she hadn't showered while she'd been held captive. Her scent was pungent to his complex senses, but Jace was convinced she was the best thing he or his wolf had ever smelled.

"Jace, do you know what you just agreed to?"

"Shh, Caleb. Let's get Sara somewhere safe so we can make sure she's okay." Sara clung tighter to him, refusing to loosen her grip long enough for him to put her in the truck. "You drive." He slid into the vehicle, keeping Sara on his lap.

"How could you just agree to what they wanted? Do you really understand what it means?"

"Shut up and drive, Caleb." He stroked Sara's hair. "I know what it means, so just be quiet." Hot tears stung his eyes, and he squeezed them shut to stop them from falling.

SARA SNUGGLED DEEPER into Jace's embrace, wishing that he and Caleb would stop snapping at each other. When the man who had taken her had snarled that he had to give her back but that things weren't over, Sara hadn't known whether to be happy or more frightened.

Then he'd grabbed her by the hair and dragged her out of the room, and fear had won out. He'd raved like a madman about pack law and rule and mates, and Sara hadn't understood any of it. Then, as she'd scrambled to keep up with him in the hallway to avoid being dragged, she'd sensed Jace and Caleb, and something had come to life inside her. Elation had bloomed. Her men had come for her. Nothing else would happen to her now that they were there to protect her.

"Jesus, what the hell did they do to her?" She flinched at Caleb's question, trying to hide the bruises that marred her flesh.

"She's fine. Just drive," Jace answered as he pulled his jacket over her and reached across the seat to turn the heat in the truck to full as shudders racked her body. Caleb growled, and Sara tensed, hating that they were fighting.

"Please don't." She managed to force the words out of her dry throat. Jace reached for a bottle of water that was in the cup holder, and Caleb glanced at her, concern shining in his eyes.

Jace unscrewed the cap and gently held the water to her lips. Sara was flooded with memories of the first time he'd given her water after saving her from hypothermia, as well as memories of her captor forcing water down her throat. The images blended together until she couldn't separate the two, and she pushed away the water he offered with a violent shove.

"No! No more!"

"Sara, it's okay. Baby, it's okay. You're safe now."

Wetness fell on Sara's cheeks, and as Jace's fingers whisked it away, she realized it was his tears, not hers. She reached up to him, cupping his cheek in her hand, desperate to reassure him that she was all right. Seeing him break apart, consumed with pain and guilt over her, felt horrible.

"So tired."

"Sleep, Sara. Just sleep. We'll wake you up when we get there."

A hush fell over the cab of the truck and lulled Sara to sleep.

* * * *

"We need to mate with her now. None of this would have happened if we had fully bonded with her. We would have been able to communicate with her and known instantly that she was in trouble." Jace paced the living room. They were back at his cabin, and he'd put Sara into his bed. He would have to move back into the town where the pack resided, but he was going to mate with Sara here before any of that happened.

"Do you think she's strong enough? It looks like they really did a number on her." They'd seen the bruising, and Sara seemed thinner than she had when she'd left them a few days ago. Leo had said she hadn't been abused, that she hadn't been forced to mate with another, but until Jace heard it from her lips, he wouldn't believe it. He didn't trust Leo as far as he could throw him.

Jace went into the bathroom and filled a bowl with warm water, his wolf screaming at him to take care of and protect their mate. He went into the bedroom and pulled back the covers, then sponged her down as he looked over her injuries.

"I'm so sorry I failed you, sweetheart. I'm so sorry I got you into this." He whispered the words against her forehead as he kissed her brow. "I can't be sorry about that deer, since it's what brought us together, but I'm so sorry for every time you've been hurt or thrown into this confusion."

"Jace?" Her voice came out soft and uncertain.

"Sara, oh sweetheart, I'm so sorry. Let us take care of you."

Caleb came into the room and lay on the bed next to Sara, cuddling her between them.

"So do one of you want to explain all this wolf and mate stuff and clue me in on why some crazy assholes broke into my house and kidnapped me?" She pressed closer to Caleb as Jace cleaned the last of the dirt from her skin.

Jace didn't know where to start. There was so much to tell her, and he didn't want to overwhelm her with too much information all at once.

"Does it hurt when you change?" she asked, filling the silence.

"No, not really. We start shifting around puberty, and it did hurt the first few times, but now it's more muscle memory than anything else. Sometimes if you fight it, it can be uncomfortable." Jace watched Sara as he gave her the answers to her questions. The fear he'd sensed from her earlier had dissipated, but she still seemed reluctant to meet his gaze as she questioned him.

"Everyone kept talking about me being your mate. What does that mean?"

Jace couldn't answer her without making eye contact, so he carefully turned her to face him before speaking. "It's like being married but deeper. Most wolves mate for life. There's a bond that grows between the mated pair, and if they've blood bonded, each biting the other, it gets to be so they crave each other. They can sense each other's emotions and sometimes their thoughts. Bonded mates will never cheat, and they'll never divorce. It's like two halves of a whole fitting together."

While Jace was speaking, Caleb rubbed soothing circles across Sara's stomach. Her gaze was guarded and troubled. "What's wrong, Sara?"

"I don't understand. How can I be your mate, then? I'm human, I'm not a wolf, and I could certainly never bite the two of you." She was so distressed that Jace hastened to reassure her.

"We believe you're meant to be mate to both of us, and we believe it's meant to be a blood bond between the three of us."

"How can you be sure? They said no one had ever mated with a human before."

Jace watched her fidget with the threads of the comforter before he covered her hands with his own.

"I knew as soon as I saw you after the accident. I took one look at you, and my wolf demanded that we claim you for our own. You remember what it was like those first few days you were here, the driving need to be together?"

Sara nodded, and her cheeks stained pink with the memory.

"You remember your reaction to my brother? It was very different from your reaction to Caleb. You bit me then. You were driven to do it, to reinforce our bond. Would it be so bad to do it again?" Jace went on, wanting her to think about how she'd reacted, instinctively biting him when confronted by his brother but not wanting her to dwell too deeply on an event that had distressed her. "When I saw the picture you'd drawn for Christmas, I knew for sure that you were meant to be ours. Maybe there's something in your lineage that allows you to mate with us. Shifters have been around for a long time. There must be a reason you had visions of both of us."

"That's why you became so distant after Christmas, isn't it? The picture, I mean."

"I didn't want you to become too attached to one of us if you were meant for both of us."

"So what happens if you mate me?"

"Caleb and I would bite you, and you would bite us as well. We would become blood bound. Committed to each other completely. It's not something that should be taken lightly."

"If you bite me, do I become a wolf too?"

Jace could feel the fear behind her question, and he gave her the most honest answer he could.

"We don't know. Normally wolves are born. It's not like what you see in the horror movies. We don't bite people to turn them into wolves, but you're the first human to mate with a lycan that we know of. It could be different for you."

"Would it hurt if you bit me?"

"There might be some discomfort, but usually the bite is done during a euphoric moment to lessen the pain."

She was quiet for a while, and Jace could almost see her mind turning the idea over. He could sense confusion from her but also apprehension. They held her between them, each stroking her gently to soothe her.

"Is it the thought of the pain that has you worried or the bond itself?" Jace asked softly.

"The pain, I guess. I mean, I want to be your mate. Everything you've described is exactly what I've imagined a relationship should be. Coming here and being with you both has shown me how cold and distant my relationships were before, but the idea of you tearing into me—I don't know if that's something I can handle even if I want the close bond with you." She shuddered in their arms.

"It isn't like that," Caleb rushed to reassure her.

"We won't attack you, Sara. We aren't going to tear into you. Biting during sex can be very erotic. Biting to initiate a bond would be even more so. Take the time to think about what you really want."

SARA'S MIND WAS reeling from Jace's revelations. Was it possible that someone in her family was a wolf? What if they bit her? Did she want to be a wolf? A lycan, as he'd called them? Did she want to be mated to the two of them? Was she ready for the deep commitment he spoke of? It was something she'd longed for when feeling the emptiness in her life, but would the reality of it be too overwhelming? She lay awake long into the night, considering what it would mean if she allowed them to bite her and bond with her fully.

Chapter Eighteen

Waiting to claim her was torture, and Caleb wanted to kick his own ass for causing the delay, but Sara needed a chance to heal both physically and mentally from her ordeal.

He also felt guilty for her being taken and couldn't bring himself to be with her while he was the one responsible for putting her in danger in the first place. He had scoured the property and the surrounding area and discovered that he was the reason the Yellow-Claw Pack had found her. Their scents lingered with his own fading trail. They'd followed him here, straight to Jace and Sara, which could only mean there were spies within the Coldridge Pack. Jace would have to be told, and Caleb knew he'd be angry. He only hoped he'd be forgiven.

The two had spoken at length about what to do about mating Sara. She wouldn't be given a reprieve now. They would have to mate her, and there would be no separation. To allow her to leave them again would mean signing her death warrant. Caleb knew she had slept fitfully the night before, trying to come to terms with everything they had revealed to her. He knew Sara was still struggling with their bonding.

It felt too close to compulsion and didn't sit well with either of them, which was why Caleb had refused to participate in claiming her until he felt she was stronger and could decide for herself.

* * * *

"Sara, we need to talk to you." Jace tried to keep the ominous tone out of his voice, not wanting to frighten her, but Imbolc was coming and the pack would expect that he return by then. They were running out of time. "I need to rejoin my pack."

"It seemed like you didn't want to do that," Sara said, placing her hand on his shoulder in a gesture of comfort. They were rocking on the porch swing, bundled up in warm winter clothes under a thick blanket, watching the moonlight bounce off the blanket of snow.

"I didn't. I don't, but when the council demands something, it's often best to fall in line."

"I know you did it to save me." Her voice was quiet, and if it hadn't been for his exceptional hearing, he might have missed what she said altogether. She turned her head away from him, and he caught the glistening of tears in her eyes.

"Hey, look at me." He waited until she turned to face him again before continuing. "I would promise them anything if it meant you were safe."

"I hate that you're in a situation you don't want to be in. You obviously left for a reason. It's clear your brother and Caleb love you, so it would have to be something awful to make you leave them, and now because of me, you have to go back."

Jace pulled her more tightly against him, tucking the blanket around them firmly, as if to cocoon them against the world. "It isn't because of you. You've done nothing wrong. It's difficult for a strong wolf, an alpha, to allow others to be in control. Our nature demands that we leave and start our own pack or that we challenge for leadership of our current pack. We fight until one of us is dead. My brother is alpha of our pack."

"That's horrible! How could they demand such a thing?"

"The lycan community isn't perfect. I wish I could say they do the things they do for a good reason, but it's only for power and the desire for more power. There are nine main packs, one for each council member, and a stronger pack means a stronger council member. Leaving to start my own pack would cause an uproar in pack structure. It's better for them if I remain in my pack, either bowing to my brother or defeating him in a challenge. They couldn't expressly forbid me to start my own pack, so this is a way of ensuring my obedience to them."

"They'll kill me if we don't mate, right? I mean, that was the gist of their threat, so what are we waiting for?"

Jace sighed. "It's not that simple. We don't want you to be mated to us because there is no other choice. That would be like living in an arranged marriage, where the people hate each other. We want you to mate with us because you love us and because you feel the need as strongly as we do. If you don't feel that way, the bonds we've already formed could be broken over time."

"I could never hate you."

"You say that now—"

"I'll say that always," Sara said, placing her hand over his mouth. "I want you. I want both of you. Do you think that's something I do every day?"

Jace pulled her hand away from his mouth and kissed her palm before tucking her hand back in her lap.

"You need to understand that we want it all. Not just to be together, not just choosing to mate—we want the deep connection that a blood bond will forge among us, and after everything you've been through, I couldn't imagine mating you."

"You don't want me anymore?"

Jace watched as her lip trembled before she sucked it between her teeth, and he realized how his words had sounded.

"They didn't hurt me. I mean, they did, but they didn't rape me, if that's why you're afraid to touch me. I'll probably hate needles after this, and going to the doctor will be...unpleasant for a while, I'm sure, but they didn't do worse than that. I'm not traumatized by the idea of sex or anything like that."

"I'm sorry. That's not what I meant at all. I just meant that I want you to enjoy your mating. I've been told it's a very intense moment, and I don't want you to be overwhelmed."

"It doesn't matter that the council have put pressure on us. I'd still want you anyway. I'd even be okay with the biting thing now that we've talked about it more, but with everyone going on about me being human and how lowly they've made that sound, I understand if you've changed your mind and would rather not."

"Damn it!" The curse slipped out before he could hold it back. Caleb wasn't here, but there was no way that he'd allow Sara to go on thinking that he didn't want her. He sent a quick mental push to Caleb to get him moving back to the cabin, pulled Sara from the swing, and carried her inside.

Clothes flew in all directions as Jace used hands and claws when necessary to get her naked as soon as possible. There was a certain type of freedom in finally being allowed to let loose with her where he'd had to be hidden before.

Once in the bedroom, he tossed her on the bed before following her down to remover her undergarments. His chilled hands made contact with her soft, warm flesh, causing her to shiver.

Jace rubbed his hands together, testing their warmth on the smooth planes of her sides, before touching her more intimately.

"Don't ever think that I don't want you, that *we* don't want you. Are you sure about the bonding?" Jace asked.

If she said no, they would hold back. They would refrain from creating a deeper bond with her than they already had. Though it wouldn't be easy, they'd do it if it was what she desired.

SARA LOOKED AT Jace, wanting him to see her conviction when she nodded. His gaze darkened, heating up with her agreement.

"Say it." His demand was rough, and he held himself away from her, as if unwilling to sway her decision.

"I want to blood bond with you." The words had barely left her lips before he grinned.

"You have no idea how happy that makes me." He growled and resumed teasing her with his touch.

Sara whimpered and arched under his calloused hands, craving more. He palmed her breasts, tugging on her hardened nipples, and she arched into him. The zing that went through her body still was not enough to quell the throbbing.

"Please," she begged, yet he still kept his distance, refusing to give her more. She didn't understand why until Caleb voiced a question from the doorway.

"Starting without me?"

"About damn time you got here!" Jace grinned in Caleb's direction. "She's hot and wet and so tight she's ready to go. I didn't think I'd be able to hold off until you got here." Jace tugged on a nipple while sucking the other into the heat of his mouth, keeping his gaze trained on Caleb almost as if taunting him.

Sara squeezed her eyes shut, overwhelmed by the lust that permeated the room. She dragged it into her lungs with every breath.

Caleb joined them on the bed, and that lust rose another notch to a nearly feverish pitch. Caleb turned her face to take her kiss while Jace continued to twirl his tongue around the turgid peak of her breast.

Caleb's tongue tangled with her own, and the pressure of his mouth made her open deeper. She groaned in disappointment when he pulled away from her, but her groan was quickly replaced by more erotic sounds as he pressed the length of his cock into her mouth. She moaned around him as Jace bit into her flesh, teasing her with the sharp edges of his teeth.

"My God, your mouth is sweet," Caleb said, pushing forward again. Sara was forced to swallow or choke on his girth.

"That's not the only thing that's sweet," Jace declared moments before lowering his head to lick at her sex.

She screamed, tearing her mouth from Caleb. "Oh please, I can't stand much more."

"We need to take you together." Caleb whispered the words to her as Jace positioned her the way he wanted. Caleb settled in front of her, draping her leg over his hip and opening her to their caress. Jace slid lubricant over her tightly puckered hole, stroking her gently when she arched back into his touch.

"Have you ever been taken here?" he asked as he probed her tender opening.

"Once, but it hurt terribly and I never wanted to try again." She shuddered as he deposited more lube inside her.

"Are you worried now?"

"Nervous, maybe. Not really worried."

"Good girl. We'd never hurt you."

THE THOUGHT OF her in bed with anyone else made the alpha in Jace see red. Where the man was intrigued, his wolf could barely stand the thought of her fucking Caleb. It was the reason Jace was going to be the first to claim her in this manner. It would appease his inner animal and make things easier for the three of them.

"Try to relax," he encouraged as Caleb slid inside her. Jace found it to be one of the most erotic things he'd ever witnessed, and instead of feeling jealousy as he had feared, he wanted her more. Wanted them both.

"That's it," he praised while he teased her with the head of his dick, pressing against her, loving the silken glide created by her flowing juices and the lubricant. He pushed a little harder, and his crown slide inside her, and Caleb retreated.

She tensed, and Jace froze, waiting for her to become accustomed to his presence.

"The pain will pass, baby. Just breathe through it," Caleb coached her, and Jace realized that he'd gone through the same thing when they made love and Caleb bottomed to him. Jace's wolf was too dominant to bottom in a relationship, but as Caleb helped Sara adjust to his invading flesh, he realized the enormous trust the two of them had placed in his hands and the degree of strength it took for them to be that open and vulnerable.

Once she began to wiggle between them and the perfume of her arousal hung in the air, Jace began moving, pistoning in and out of her in a smooth, controlled motion. Once they were sure she was used to it, he paused, holding still so Caleb could enter her pussy.

Sara groaned and hissed but soon rocked her hips against them, drawing them each deeper into her in turn. Jace opened his mental link with Caleb, sharing not only what he was feeling but also his intended movements and rhythm.

They moved together, pushing Sara steadily toward release. As she clung between them, Jace could feel their release coming.

"Sara, will you allow us to form a blood one with you?" He prepared for it, nudging Sara's neck to the side and brushing her hair out of his way as Caleb did the same on the other side of her neck. He felt her tighten around him.

"Do it," Sara wailed, her body convulsing on him again.

"*Now!* he urged Caleb, and they struck at the same time, fangs sinking into her where neck and shoulder met. She climaxed in a flood of hot arousal and clenching muscles.

Jace raised his head from her neck, as did Caleb. They struck at each other's throats, inflicting similar wounds. When they had taken enough to form a mating bond with each other as well as with Sara, they encouraged her to drink at their wounds and were surprised when she licked enthusiastically at their wounds, offering no resistance to a custom that was completely foreign to her. She drank from first Jace and then Caleb before sinking back into the mattress, totally replete.

AS SHE LAY there, memories that were not her own started to swirl through her mind. She felt love and affection for Caleb and knew it came from Jace since it was much deeper than what she'd begun to feel for the man.

She wondered what she was broadcasting to them and for a moment was terribly embarrassed. She tried to pull in on herself to close herself off, and Jace spoke up.

"Please don't. Not yet. I know it's scary, but we'll all learn to stay out of each other's minds and respect each other's privacy. This is such a new and intimate moment. Please let us all feel it fully."

Chapter Nineteen

Almost as if they were being watched, Jace was summoned home the day after their mating. It put a damper on the euphoric feelings that had swamped them in the hours after their mating.

They had stayed up late into the night loving each other, and Jace was exhausted now. They had tried to help Sara forge the mental bonds of communication with them, but it seemed after their initial sharing that it was beyond her, at least for the time being. Jace suspected she placed the limitation on herself just by believing she couldn't do it, but he didn't know how to overcome the issue.

"Don't worry, love. I'm sure it will come in time," Caleb had encouraged her, kissing the tip of her nose. Jace wasn't sure it would happen since she was human, but he tucked that thought into the deepest part of his mind, hiding it away from Sara for now so he wouldn't hurt her feelings. They would have to discuss it eventually, but she had endured so much that he hated the thought of overwhelming her.

He also tried to hide his growing anxiety about rejoining the pack, but he was sure both Sara and Caleb could feel his distress.

As if confirming his suspicions, Sara caught him in a tight hug and Caleb laid a kiss against the corner of his mouth. "It will be okay," Caleb offered after pulling away. "We'll get through it together."

The pack lived in a town a few hundred miles away, and in the snow the drive took several hours. The three of them were quiet the entire drive, and the tension grew to an unbearable level.

Jace expected the tension to extend to when they reached the town, but the pack was in an uproar.

Jace raced toward his brother's house, the pungent scent of smoke clinging to the air. "What the hell is going on?" Jace yelled over the din.

Several pack members had shifted and were tracking while others remained in human form to get the women and pups to safety. There was a time when the females would have fought fiercely alongside the men, but with fewer women, the pack's survival instincts demanded they be protected.

"Some of our homes have been attacked, burned to the ground. Leo and two of the other council members are dead. It smells like Yellow-Claw Pack and another scent we haven't been able to identify."

"What do you need?" He fell in step with Ryan, only shortening his stride when Sara struggled to keep up.

"Right now I need you to track and later use your medical skills to help tend the wounded. Caleb can help get everyone to safety."

"Sara, go with Caleb. He'll keep you safe." He pressed a quick kiss to her lips and then to Caleb's. "I love you," he said, turning away, and he followed his brother.

* * * *

Tracking had taken several hours, and seeing to the wounded had taken even longer. Now only the most severe injuries remained, lycan physiology having taken care of the rest.

He was near to dropping when his brother joined him. "I fear this is only the beginning. I don't know what the Yellow-Claw Pack hoped to gain with the stunt they pulled here, but people are dead. This isn't a game. They've started a war. Hell, I'd like to kill them for what they did to Sara alone," Jace spoke, forgetting in the heat of the moment that he wasn't pack leader and was supposed to bow to his brother.

Fortunately Ryan seemed to take his comment for what it was rather than the challenge it could be perceived as. "Go home, Jace. You've done more than your share, and you're exhausted. Go home to Sara and Caleb."

The mention of his mates brought a smile to his face, and his brother smirked. "So mated to two people, and one of them human no less. You never did anything the easy way."

"Maybe not, but I'm happy," he said, realizing how true it was. He was happy even here. He just hoped it lasted.

Walking into his old home was strange. Everything was just as he'd left it but different somehow, maybe because he was different. He didn't know for sure, but he felt a certain level of discord that only dissipated when he entered his bedroom to see Sara and Caleb curled together in his bed, moonlight spilling over their bodies, making them seem ethereal. He wanted to go to them, to claim his rightful place in this bed with his mates, but the pungent smell of charred wood and death clung to his skin, and he wouldn't soil either of them with such filth.

As quietly as he could, Jace padded down to the bathroom. He barely let the water warm in the shower before stepping in. As exhausted as he was, his natural barriers were coming down, and he was catching the very erotic images Sara was dreaming.

They were enough to make him blush. He tried to restore her privacy, erecting a barrier between their minds, but it was almost impossible as she dreamed of Jace taking Caleb while she pleasured Caleb on her knees in the perfect subservient position.

She looked up at him in the dream through her lashes, and Jace gripped himself in the shower to keep from coming against the tiled wall. He slammed the barrier closed between them quickly, twisting the cold-water tap in the shower and letting icy water pound over him as he tried to forget what she'd been dreaming.

Once he had himself under control, he stepped from the shower, toweled off, and slipped into bed beside them, smiling as he realized that Sara could share with them, confirming that it was only her conscious mind that kept her distant from them. He'd been so engrossed with the erotic images she'd been broadcasting that he hadn't focused on how clearly she'd been able to transmit the message.

Chapter Twenty

Preparations for Imbolc were under way. The rubble from the burned houses had been cleared, and the pack was pulling together to fix what they could and rebuild the rest. There had been talk of postponing the celebration, but most felt it was too important to forgo the ritual, especially since there was a full moon this Imbolc.

Sara watched the large bonfire being built in the town square. Jace and Caleb had explained that there would be dancing around the fire after the pack hunted together. She knew Jace worried about how she would view the hunt, afraid that she would think their customs were savage. The only thing she really worried about, though, was not fitting in.

Sara wasn't sure, but she feared Leo being dead might mean that Jace didn't have to remain mated to her, and she worried that being human, she wouldn't be able to join in the festivities as fully as the others.

Jace had told her there would be a great feast and dancing and howling at the moon. She wasn't sure if he was joking about that last part, but she would bet he wasn't.

As the afternoon faded, the pack set out to hunt. They were after deer, and the strangest sensation crept over Sara as she watched them head out, shifting seamlessly into their lycan forms. She was filled with awe and just a touch of envy when the feeling of guilt swept in, and it wasn't her guilt.

Her gaze snapped to Jace, who regarded her sheepishly. They were still getting a handle on controlling the mental spillover from one another and sometimes got snippets not meant for them.

"Why should the thought of hunting deer make you feel so guilty?"

"The day we met, I was hunting a deer." He said nothing else, as if waiting for her to put the pieces together.

"Oh, oh—you mean the deer I nearly hit? The one that caused my accident?"

"I didn't mean for it to happen."

Sara could feel his pain as if it were her own. She felt his fear upon finding her half frozen in the snow, but she couldn't be mad at him. He hadn't meant to hurt her, and she couldn't regret what had brought them together.

She laughed, snuggling into his embrace before shoving him away from her. "Go hunt."

"You're not angry?"

"Not even a little. Now go bag a deer," she encouraged him.

Once he'd left with the rest of the pack, Sara was uncertain what to do. She wanted to be useful. She wanted to make Jace and Caleb proud. She wanted to be accepted by the pack, but she didn't know how to make that happen, so she did the only thing she could think of. She cooked.

There was already a ton of food, but the table seemed a little light in the dessert area, so Sara made cakes and pies, custards, and brownies until she was sure that she had enough to feed the entire pack.

They were gone for hours, and Sara started to wonder when they'd be back. She tried to keep her jealousy at bay. She'd noticed that even though there were very few women in the pack, they were all gorgeous and many of them had eyes that stayed glued to Jace and Caleb. She had no doubt that a lot of the women wanted them.

She'd felt their eyes on her too since they'd been here, but Jace and Caleb only had eyes for her. It helped assuage her insecurity, but she was sure it would lead to tension between her and the other members of the pack.

Sara knew the men fought, challenging each other for dominance and positions in the pack, but was unsure how to assert her position in the pack if she was truly to be part of it. How to bring it up to Jace, or even Caleb, posed another problem. They had been different when they were all alone at the cabin. Jace had told her the shifter community valued power, but she hadn't grasped how completely. She didn't want Jace or Caleb to view her differently but wasn't certain how she would handle a challenge by one of the lycan females. She would have to tell Jace or Caleb, but she would have to find the right way and the right time so they didn't feel any guilt about her giving up her life to be with them.

* * * *

The house smelled amazing when Jace and Caleb came in around dinnertime. It smelled like a home to Jace for the first time in a long time. Every available surface was covered in baked goods that Sara had spent the afternoon laboring over.

The pack had caught a deer that would be cooked for the next feast, there was a deer they'd previously caught already roasting, and they would enjoy Sara's desserts. She'd outdone herself making sure the entire pack would have something, and she looked cute covered in flour and powdered sugar. Jace wanted to lick her clean.

"You didn't have to go to all this trouble," Jace said.

"I wanted to do something nice for you."

"You certainly set the bar high," Caleb said. He swiped a finger through the sugar crystals on her cheek before sucking the tip of his finger between his lips. "Are you ready for tonight? It's going to be epic."

"Are you nervous?" Jace asked, carefully watching the expression on her face as she fussed over the numerous dishes she'd prepared.

"You can't read my mind?" She gave an anxious laugh.

"I probably could if I tried, but we give each other as much privacy as we can. It can be disconcerting to have someone else walking through your thoughts all the time."

"I'm nervous," she admitted. "I don't know how I'll fit in."

"It's a party. One of our greatest celebrations. Don't worry about fitting in—just worry about having fun," Caleb said.

Jace nodded in agreement. "Just relax and have a good time." He watched as Caleb took the dish she'd been toying with and marched it out the back door. Jace followed his lead, grabbing a plate of the cookies Sara had made.

"I'll try," she said, laughing nervously again. She followed him, her own hands full of baked goods.

"Come look around before things get crowded," Jace suggested.

"What about the rest of the food?" she asked, glancing back at the house.

"Someone else can bring out the rest, or we'll finish up later," Caleb reassured her, gesturing toward the many people setting up for the party. They led her away from where the food was being set up to a large, sheltered grove of trees where the trees were ancient and their roots ran deep.

"This is our most sacred space. The pack has gathered here for generations for all of our celebrations." Jace watched as she wandered around the clearing, touching the trees and allowing her fingertips to caress the smoothly worn stone.

"It's breathtaking."

Chapter Twenty-One

Sara could feel the reverence of the gathering and couldn't resist touching as much of her surroundings as she could. The tree in front of her stretched toward the sky, its many limbs reminding her of an octopus. She doubted that the entire pack would be able to encompass its great width. Touching the tree wasn't enough, and she laid her cheek against the bark, anxious to hear its secrets.

Embarrassed and feeling guilty for having touched without permission, she pulled her hand away and stepped back, glancing at Jace. "I'm sorry. It's just hard to ignore how powerful this place feels."

Jace smiled at her before placing her hand back against the bark of the tree. "It's a little like being in a museum and wanting to touch the beauty behind the velvet ropes, isn't it?"

Sara nodded and once again let her fingertips caress the rough trunk of the tree. "Yes, that's it exactly."

Once the party started, Sara forgot about her nervousness. The trip to the clearing, feeling the energy of the space, had calmed her. The celebration was fun and loud, like swirling lights and colors. Someone put on music. The heavy bass vibrated through her, and Sara found herself swaying to the beat.

Sara felt the gazes of others on her, but she pushed that out of her mind, focusing instead on the food that was placed on long wooden tables in front of them. The entire pack raised a toast and then waited for Ryan to begin eating.

Sara watched with fascination as all the members around the table deferred to Ryan, each seemingly ready for any whim he might express. Caleb had explained the how pack priority worked and how the pack would behave so that they showed proper respect to their alpha. It was fascinating to see how the pack as a whole treated Ryan. The behavior was uniform throughout the group. Sara picked up small clues into the dynamics of each couple. She watched in amazement as it became apparent which members were dominant and who was more comfortable in a beta role. When Caleb had described to her what the pack was like, she'd assumed that the males would hold the alpha positions among the couples. She was surprised to find that wasn't always the case. Even the children seemed to have their own hierarchy, and she bit her lip to keep from laughing as she watched a young girl put the boy sitting next to her in his place when he reached for the mashed potatoes before her.

Sara waited to grab her own plate until after both Jace and Caleb had begun to eat, silently showing them that she ranked them above herself and that she would defer to them. She noticed how closely the women of the pack watched their interactions and finally understood what Caleb meant when he'd explained that it would help her standing in the pack to show a proper amount of respect. Although the females also held a certain amount of reverence for Ryan, it was clear that their own structure was in a state of upheaval. Jace had told her about Hayley and her breakup with Ryan and explained how that had left a hole in the hierarchy among the women.

There was a lot about lycans that she didn't understand. While she knew only the alpha pair in a natural wolf pack mated, that obviously wasn't the case with lycans. Mated couples sat together, and Sara recognized the bonds they shared as something similar to the one she shared with Caleb and Jace.

Many of the pack watched the interaction among the three of them, focusing specifically on Sara. She was an oddity they didn't understand. The scrutiny made her uncomfortable, and she shifted closer to Caleb and Jace. They both smiled at her, sending warmth down through their mental connection to her.

After the meal there was more dancing, this time around the fire, and the drumbeats pounded into the earth and seemed to connect them all together. The sense of family astounded Sara, and she was glad to be a part of it, even if she hadn't fully integrated within the pack.

When it came time to pay homage to the moon, all the lycans shifted. She was surrounded by wolves of many different sizes and colors. They threw back their heads in unison and howled, their voices ringing out across the night in joyous song.

It made her sad that she couldn't join them, but she could feel the beams of light caressing her skin, almost as if the moon itself accepted her. The howling continued for a long time, and then the crowd thinned out, some staying in wolf form and some shifting back to human.

She watched as several couples embraced. Heat colored her cheeks as their touching became more intimate, their embraces more erotic. It made her long for her own mates, desire to feel their touch. They came to her as if sensing her need.

"We've done our duty. Let's go home and have our own celebration," Jace suggested.

"What, no dancing?"

"We'll dance at home," Caleb said, taking her hand to lead her away from the ritual area. The time for ceremony was over, though, and now her men had another kind of celebration planned.

She let them take her from the party, anticipation turning in her stomach so that a sensation close to butterfly wings fluttered against her ribs.

"You've been dreaming naughty things, sweetheart," Caleb accused.

"Mmm. Time to make some of those naughty dreams a reality," Jace said, wrapping his arm around her shoulder as they walked toward the house.

JACE WAS GROWING impatient, so he swept her into his arms and carried her the rest of the way to the house. She giggled when he carried her across the threshold. The symbolism wasn't lost on him, and it seemed fitting, given that they were mated, linked together stronger than any human marriage could make them. It gave him a thrill to do something normal, something that represented a custom of traditional commitment.

His impatience was fueled by the numerous dreams she'd been having, each hotter than the last. His mate was an imaginative woman with a deep range of desires, and they played out in her sleep in great detail. Now, on one of their most sacred holidays, he intended to make one of her dreams come true.

It seemed that Sara was fascinated with his relationship with Caleb, and since they'd mated, she'd only been with one or the other or between them. Tonight he would mix things up.

Once they were in the house, they stripped her bare and took her into the shower, where they cleaned her with painstaking care before finally bathing themselves. Jace had opened the link between him and Caleb, communicating what he intended for them, making sure that Caleb and his wolf were okay with how things would play out. Jace could feel Caleb's rising excitement as they prepared.

When they took her into the bedroom, she automatically stretched out on her back in the middle of the mattress, and while they would both spend a long time preparing her, making sure she was ready for everything they would do to her, Jace tsked, his tongue clicking against the roof of his mouth, as he moved her to the side of the bed.

"Not yet, baby." He and Caleb pulled off the towels they had wrapped around their waists, revealing themselves to her and chuckling as she gasped, her breath catching in her throat. "For now you watch, so get comfortable." Jace propped a pillow behind her head, ensuring she had a good view of the show he was about to put on for her.

Once he was sure she was watching, he caught Caleb by his neck and pulled him in until their lips met. It started as a soft kiss but quickly became open-mouthed, tongues tangling. When he pulled away again, he brought his lips to the pulse point in Caleb's neck, licking over the steady beat of his heart and letting his teeth graze the surface. Caleb and Sara groaned together, spurring him on.

They stretched out on the bed next to her, and Jace let his hands run over Caleb's muscles. He scraped the blunt tips of his nails across Caleb's buttocks and listened to Sara's breathing change.

"Touch yourself," Jace ordered, pausing to look at Sara as Caleb leaned over him to take him in his mouth. Jace threw back his head with a hiss, enjoying the heat and suction that Caleb drew him in with.

The air was thick with the scent of Sara's arousal, and Jace turned his head to watch her as she fondled herself.

"That's it, baby. Pull those nipples for us." They watched as she tugged and twisted her hips, rising off the bed searching for a caress. "We're a little busy. You're going to have to do it on your own, at least for a little while."

Caleb took him to the back of his throat, and Sara ran her hand between her legs, spreading the wetness Jace could see glistening there.

"Yes!" It slipped out as a hiss, and Jace wasn't sure who he was encouraging, but as his abdominal muscles tightened with his impending release, he knew he had to move things along.

He moved out of Caleb's reach and grabbed the lube he'd set on the nightstand. Caleb had been in this situation many times and knew what was coming, so he moved into the position Jace wanted.

"Okay, sweetheart, now it's your turn," Caleb encouraged Sara, pulling her toward him. Jace smiled as she spread her legs for Caleb, welcoming him into her body. Jace took a moment to watch as Caleb claimed her.

Chapter Twenty-Two

Once Caleb was fully seated and moving in a regular rhythm, Jace used the lube to ease his way into Caleb's body, loving the tight clasp of flesh. He moved carefully, aware that their combined weight could crush Sara and to give Caleb time to adjust to his thrusts.

The links between them opened fully, and it was as if they were one being with one set of emotions. He could feel himself as he pushed into Caleb. He could feel the stretch and burn his invasion caused Caleb, and he could feel the snug fit of Sara around Caleb as he struggled to hold back his release.

SARA CRIED OUT as she came, falling apart completely. She'd never experienced anything like she'd felt when she was watching them. They were perfect, and they had crawled into her heart and made a home there. She couldn't imagine being without them ever again. She basked in the afterglow of her climax, relaxed as they ran their hands over her body until the smell of smoke assaulted their nostrils. It seemed the reprieve they'd expected for Imbolc wasn't granted after all. The Yellow-Claw Pack truly wanted to start a war.

The smoke was thicker in the air than it had been when they first arrived in town a few days ago. At first Sara thought the bonfire had gotten out of control. She almost hoped that it had—that would mean the fire was an accident and not another set by the pack that had kidnapped her. Sara shuddered, unable to stop the disgust that swept through her at the thought of being at their mercy.

It quickly became obvious that the bonfire wasn't to blame. It had been extinguished hours ago, and the surrounding area was unblemished. The same couldn't be said for the outer edge of the town, or an area to the east that had been engulfed in fire.

Ryan sent out another search party, but they were unable to find anything more than the scent of the ones who had set the fires. Some were the same as last time, but not all, and it became clear to her that the lycans had a severe problem.

Security was amped up around town, and Sara began to feel like a prisoner. Jace and Caleb demanded she stay with one of them at all times, and the pack cut off her communication with the outside world. While she'd expected her movements to be monitored while she gained the trust of the pack, she hadn't expected them to cut her off from everything she'd known. It felt like being indoctrinated into a cult, and as the days wore on after Imbolc, Sara felt more and more lonely. She doubted she'd be able to hide it from Jace or Caleb for very long. For the first time, the mating and its side effects seemed like a horrible idea.

* * * *

"Hey, beautiful," Jace said, kissing her. He could see sadness lurking in her gaze, and the feelings he was catching from their shared link were confused and in turmoil. He felt her withdraw into herself, and their connection wavered.

"Hey, hey, what's wrong?" Jace knew she'd been cut off from her life, but he worried she wouldn't tell him what she was thinking or feeling. He knew she was often stoic and could sense how she held her emotions in check, as if trying to behave in a way that he expected. He could already feel the fragile strands of their bond stretching past what they were meant to, and he worried that if he pushed, those threads would snap. He wondered what would happen if he didn't press her for an answer. Maintaining harmony required a delicate balance that he hadn't expected would be necessary.

"It's nothing, really. It's all just been a very big change, and I can't help feeling completely useless. At least at the cabin I could take pictures and submit them for work. Now I can't get near my camera, much less a computer, without someone wondering if

I'm going to sell a story about werewolves to some trash tabloid." She sniffed loudly, as if holding back tears. It was like a blade through his heart.

Jace let the feelings trickle through to Caleb, knowing that the three of them needed to have this discussion together. It didn't take long before Caleb came striding through the door with a sense of authority that Jace hadn't seen in him before their mating to Sara.

It was as if she had awoken the alpha within Caleb. Jace would be alpha to them all, but Caleb would be her alpha as well. Nature had chosen for them, but it seemed that Sara wasn't entirely happy with nature's choice.

"What's wrong?" Caleb asked, his voice hiding an edge of panic that made Jace cringe.

"See, this is exactly the kind of thing I mean!" Sara yelled before hunching in on herself as if hiding from them both. "I'm not like you. I don't belong here!"

Caleb shot him an accusatory look before coming to stand in front of Sara. Jace shrugged, bewildered by her outpouring of emotions. Jace watched Caleb, his heaving chest nearly brushing Sara's bent head, the dark waves of her hair trembling as she struggled to get hold of her emotions.

"Sara, you do belong here. You belong with us." The deep timber of Caleb's statement revealed the pain the other man was trying to hide. Pain that echoed his own. Now that they were together, he couldn't imagine losing either of them.

A look of determination and resolve turned Sara's normally warm honey-brown eyes hard and cold. "I can't be something I'm not. I'm not a good fit here."

"You are. Don't you see you're the perfect fit with us?" Caleb grabbed her by the shoulders as if to shake some sense into her, causing Jace to growl.

"Let her go, Caleb." His words were low but full of authority that Caleb couldn't deny and wouldn't disobey.

"I wasn't going to hurt her. I'd never hurt her. I can't believe you're just going to let her walk out! What happens to us then? What happens to us when she's gone, taking our only chance for a mate with her?" Caleb jerked his hands away from Sara, as if touching her had burned him.

"What the hell is he talking about?" Sara asked around hiccups as tears streamed down her cheeks. She swiped furiously at the tears as they continued to fall.

"Sara, it's not in our nature to give up something that's ours, and you are ours whether that sounds sexist or possessive or not. Those are human terms, human concepts that mean nothing to the animal that both Caleb and I have inside us. We would kill for you. We would die for you. We only want you to be happy."

Jace knew his words were intense, and he didn't want to frighten her, but it was important that she understand their nature.

"We've mated, and it will hurt to break the bond with us. I'm not sure it's completely safe even with Leo dead, but we can try if that's what you want." The other members of the council might trust her enough to keep their secret and let her go, but it was still a gamble. The mating bond posed another variable, and Jace didn't know how Sara would respond to being separated from them.

HER THROAT FELT like it was going to close and her chest was on fire. She'd never imagined that they would let her walk away. She assumed that they would put up more of a fight. That they didn't made her heart feel as if someone were squeezing it in a vise.

"Isn't there any way you could give me some space? You know, time to get used to things?" The thought that they would abandon her completely was almost too much to bear. "Does it have to be all or nothing?" Her voice quivered on the last word, making her feel weak.

"No, of course not!" The words exploded out of Caleb's mouth, but it wasn't just him she needed a response from. Looking to Jace, she could see him gathering his control, shoring up his resolve before he spoke.

"No, but you have to understand that you have to decide what you really want. We can only exist in limbo for so long before it's like pulling the tail of a wild animal. You mated with us, blood bonded with us. Breaking that connection will be extremely painful. Even scaling it back to something more closely resembling a human relationship or marriage will be difficult. If you haven't made a choice about what you need from us, if you wait too long, our instincts — our nature — will demand we reclaim you because you're our mate and you're meant to be with us."

* * * *

The three of them agreed on two weeks. During that time, she would think about what it really meant to be with them, and they would help Ryan sort out the problems within the pack. She knew their hope was that it would be safer and she'd be afforded more freedom, but Sara wasn't so sure it would be like that. Since her arrival, very few pack members had tried to make her feel welcome, and it seemed that the single women of the pack were more interested in viewing her as competition than befriending her. They couldn't fathom that two of their strongest males would settle for a human, and it seemed that, despite the fact that there was little choice in who mated whom, Sara's bonding with Jace and Caleb was viewed as more of an oddity rather than a true mating. There were a few who poked at Sara, almost as if testing the strength of her connection with the men. It made Sara worry what would happen if she stayed away too long.

It had only been a few hours before Sara started to become restless. Caleb and Jace had warned her to expect withdrawal symptoms from severing their connection so abruptly. She had assumed they'd been exaggerating.

"It's going to be hard for all of us, Sara, but I would expect that you'll bear the brunt of the pain. Normally we would be able to be apart and only experience mild discomfort after extended absences from each other. The link to each other helps to reassure each other."

She'd had no idea that the physical signs would hit so fast. The headache hit her like a hammer between the eyes, clawing at her temples and making her jaw throb. Anxiety hit her hard next until she feared her heart would pound out of her chest and her ribs felt like they were breaking while she tried to pull air into her lungs. When the chills came, she cranked up the heat in her house. The sweats made her shiver, and before long mood swings started.

She could sense both men reaching out for her. She could tell they were trying to comfort her even through their own pain. It was subtle at first, but she felt it all the same, and while it helped with some of the physical symptoms of missing them, it didn't help with her mood.

The second day, Sara started cleaning the entire house, unable to sit still. She was still completely displaced in her house. It was as if it belonged to someone else, and she almost called the guys to come get her, but she held back, feeling like she owed it to them and to herself to fully consider what it would mean for the three of them if she were to come back.

Sara tried to distract herself with work. There was a new magazine looking for specialized nature articles complete with photography. It was perfect. Sara read over the requirements for submission, ready to send in her résumé and apply for a freelance position on the spot.

Pushing aside her discomfort, she focused on updating her portfolio. It took her several hours to choose from the nature photos she had, selecting several she'd taken at Jace's cabin. Sara had shoved her emotions down so many times that when there was a knock on her door that afternoon, she was ready to bite the head off of whoever was on the other side. She was shaky and irritable, and when she looked through the peephole and saw who it was, she seriously considered ignoring him and crawling back into her bed.

"Come on, Sara. I know you're home. I saw your shadow fall across the door." Nate knocked again and again until Sara finally threw open the door.

"What are you doing here?" Sara couldn't keep the anger out of her voice.

"I just want to talk. Can I come in?"

The urge to refuse was strong, but Sara didn't have any reason to believe that Nate would hurt her, and he still had belongings in the house that she had no right to deny him.

Almost as if sensing that her resolve was weakening, Nate pushed again. "Come on. I just want to talk. You know me. I'm not going to hurt you," he said, and a giggle threatened to escape as she clenched her teeth together. She'd become so accustomed to Jace and Caleb sensing her thoughts or emotions, and for a split second it seemed as if Nathan could too.

The urge to laugh evaporated quickly as she called out to him. "You've already hurt me." The image of him with another woman in their bed was still fresh in her mind, though if she were honest with herself, it wasn't as painful as it had been before she'd spent time with Caleb and Jace. Sara stepped aside to allow him entrance.

"Thank you." He smiled, and Sara wanted to smack the smug look right off his face.

"Don't thank me. Just say what you came to say and get whatever crap you came to get so you can leave again." Sara crossed her arms under her breasts and then instantly shifted position when Nate's dirty gaze was drawn there. She cleared her throat loudly in an obvious attempt to draw his gaze up toward her face.

"I was wrong. I wanted to tell you how sorry I am."

"What's wrong? Did she kick you to the curb already?"

"What? No!"

She could see the look on his face, though, and while he tried for a sincere expression, he couldn't fully hide his embarrassment. The redhead had obviously had enough of Nate. Sara just wasn't sure what his angle was here.

"You know we were good together."

Nate reached for her. His hand on her shoulder felt like razor blades being dragged over her skin. When he moved as if to cup the side of her neck in a more intimate embrace, Sara thought she would scream. She clamped her teeth together to hold back the sound of her discomfort. Confused at how much pain he'd inflicted, she maneuvered away from him so he couldn't do it again.

"You lost any right you had to touch me," she said, trying to sort through her turmoil. He hadn't intended to hurt her. He hadn't actually done anything that should have caused pain, and yet it had.

He looked angry at her words, finally seeming to realize that her days of trying to please him were over, but fortunately he didn't try to touch her again. Sara could still feel the sensation of his hand on her like fire ants on her skin. She had felt the press of both Caleb and Jace in the moment, and it had taken everything she possessed to block them out, but doing so felt incredibly unnatural. She wanted their touch, craved their comfort, and she could feel their hurt when she pushed them away. It made something inside her weep.

"If you don't want me, would you at least consider continuing to do photos for the website? I know they approached you to stay, and your stuff is so good. We can't afford to lose the talent. There have been fires north of here, and the magazine wants to do a piece on Bigfoot."

It took her a moment to realize that the fires he spoke of were the same fires Jace and Caleb had been dealing with. They had nothing to do with Bigfoot, but they did have something to do with werewolves. What Nate might find if he started looking into the fire and searching for Bigfoot, poking around and sticking his nose where it didn't belong, made her heart give a hard, heavy thump.

"Bigfoot? Seriously?" She laughed nervously, but Nate didn't seem to notice. Sara tried to keep her voice even, despite the panic trying to tear a hole through her throat.

"You won't even consider it?"

The idea of taking pictures and having steady work did appeal to her, but the idea of putting Jace and Caleb or their pack in danger or ever working with Nate again did not. But Nate knew her, and she knew if she made too much of a stink about Bigfoot being a hoax, she'd tip him off that something was up with the story. If that happened, he'd dig more and keep digging until he found something.

"Come on. It will be like old times. Trust can be rebuilt if you let it. Don't you miss what we were at all?"

"Nate, you slept with another woman. In our bed. That trust can't be rebuilt. We're done. While I appreciate the confidence in my work and that you're trying to be a professional about things, I've moved on."

"Moved on? You're seeing someone?" Shock and anger were evident in his tone, and it made her own anger rise in response.

"What right do you have to question me? You're the one who ruined what we had. What do you care if I'm seeing someone else now?"

"So that's it, then. You're just going to throw it all away? Over me and under someone else already." Nate put his hand on her shoulder, and it was all she could do to stifle the scream that was desperate to escape so that it came out in a frustrated grunt rather than the ear-piercing screech she wanted to unleash on him.

"Are you not listening? We're already done. I'm not throwing anything away, and you need to leave now. I'll send your things to you. Don't come back here." Sara stepped away from him, giving him a wide path to the door, feeling dirty that he'd touched her again.

He turned as if to say more, but her patience finally snapped, and with a parting growl that would have made both her alpha males proud, she slammed the door in his face.

"Sara, are you all right?" The thought floated through her mind clearly in Jace's voice. Sara had no idea how to answer him with words, so she tried to send the impression that she was fine. The last thing she wanted was for Jace or Caleb to come rushing in to save her. She had no doubt that there would be an altercation if they came face to face with Nate.

"We can come to you." This time, Caleb's voice.

Sara knew she had to try harder to communicate with them. *"I'm fine. I don't need you to come to me."* She sent soothing feelings, trying to put them at ease, finally sending the impression of safety as she locked her door.

Once she was alone, the reactions that she'd had to Nate's touch faded, but the symptoms she'd experienced since leaving Caleb and Jace reasserted themselves with a vengeance, nearly buckling her knees. Although she was adamant that she would stay away from the men until she was sure she wanted a relationship with them, even if it meant dealing with pack politics and shared feelings she struggled to understand, it was clear what her body wanted. She only hoped that her heart and mind decided quickly.

Chapter Twenty-Three

"Why would you let her leave?"

Jace snorted at Ryan's question. "I think you'll find 'let' doesn't factor in when you find your mate. You'll realize that it becomes paramount to keep her happy, and you'll do anything to make and keep her that way."

"Jace, the council is still up in arms about her, about you mating a human. You were told to keep her here!"

"She's not a prisoner! We couldn't force her to stay."

"They will kill her. You get that, right? In order to keep our secret, they'll kill her, and then you'll want to die right along with her. Why the hell would you allow her to go? It must be driving you insane to be away from her."

"You have no idea. It helps to have Caleb around though. I don't think I'd be able to stay away if it was just the two of us bonded, but being with Caleb makes it at least somewhat bearable." Jace felt strange admitting how he was feeling to his brother.

"I'm glad being with Caleb has made things easier for you, but have you considered how Sara is feeling? She has no one. It must be harder for her. Jace, you need to bring her back here. I can't hold off the council members forever. Bring her home, brother, and solidify her place with us."

Jace couldn't admit to Ryan that the separation might not be permanent. He was fighting an internal battle with his inner wolf, and the animal wouldn't allow him to admit that he'd given up dominance to Sara.

Ryan didn't say "or else" when he instructed Jace to bring her back into the fold, but Jace knew there would be trouble if he didn't comply. He just couldn't bring himself to make Sara stay if she didn't want to.

* * * *

A full week passed. It was longer than they had ever thought Sara would last, and they were going out of their minds. Jace had no idea what to do with the perpetual erection he had — even shifting didn't take away the immense need. He and Caleb had agreed they wouldn't sleep together without Sara, so that solution was off the table, and even though having Caleb close to him helped, he was ready to fall on his knees and beg Sara to come back to them, no longer caring if that made him submissive to his mate. Both he and his wolf would come to terms with it if she agreed to return.

The attacks on the town had stopped at least momentarily, Jace assumed it was because the Yellow-Claw Pack didn't want to attract too much unwanted attention from the outside world. Too many fires would bring outsiders into the area, and officials would begin to suspect arson and foul play. No matter what their agenda was, the pack wouldn't risk that kind of exposure.

The break from their arson problem meant that Jace was able to focus more energy on why the Yellow-Claw Pack had taken Sara and what the council would have had to gain by not returning her immediately when they'd discovered the Yellow-Claws had taken a human and were holding her against her will.

That night Ryan called a pack meeting to discuss the Yellow-Claw Pack and the troubles they'd been having.

"Where's the human?" one of his pack members yelled from the back of the room. His tone had Jace clenching his fists, desperate to take a swing at him.

"Sara is still adjusting to life with us." Ryan stressed her name, holding up his hand for silence as a rumble went through the crowd gathered there. "I've gathered you here to discuss other pressing matters. We have to find a way to stop the Yellow-Claw Pack before their destruction spreads even further through the lycan community. I have reached out to the Redwoods in an attempt to form an alliance with our brothers and sisters to stop this fighting before we have a full-blown civil war on our hands. It's gone on long enough, and we can't risk drawing the attention of humans."

"Yet you bring one among us!"

"I want to know why they took her." Jace's voice was strong when he spoke up.

"Would you have let another pack member bring a human here? Or is it just favoritism you show for your brother?"

"Would one of you like to bring a formal challenge instead of heckling from the crowd?" The full power of the alpha line filled Ryan's voice, sending a ripple through the group. Some whined low in their throats, their gazes going to the floor in gestures of submission. Other, weaker pack members actually sank to the floor, crouching low to show subservience.

Jace bowed his head as a sign of respect, but the urge to submit didn't have him squirming in his seat. He was an alpha in his own right and suspected the power he could draw through their line would rival what his brother was able to produce.

When no one issued a challenge, Ryan continued. "It will take time to discover why the Yellow-Claws had such as strong interest in Sara. I can only assume it is because their own fertility issues have grown dire."

After that Sara was forgotten as a topic, and the meeting went on. They spoke of defense strategy against the Yellow-Claws, disciplinary action, and what to do about the depleted council. The meeting was nearly finished when Jace was overcome with anguish that nearly brought him to his knees.

"Are you all right?" Caleb asked, using their mental link to each other and taking Jace's weight.

"We need to get out of here." Sweat beaded on Jace's forehead, and he bit back a groan.

"What's wrong?"

"It's not me. We have to go to Sara." Searing pain radiated through him as he felt convulsions tear through her until there was nothing but cool, empty darkness.

* * * *

Once the feeling of quiet the darkness brought settled inside him, it was easier to think, but it was difficult to think of anything but Sara.

"Drive faster, Caleb."

"Do you want to get pulled over?"

"No, but drive faster. Please, we need to get to Sara. All I could feel was pain, and now I can't feel her at all. Please go!" Everything inside Jace demanded that he get out of the car and run to Sara as quickly as he could. He knew he couldn't, though. As fast as he was, the car was faster. Not being able to feel or sense Sara was driving him crazy and had his heckles up, but he tried desperately to hold himself together.

"Can you feel her? Can you feel anything from her, Caleb?" Jace asked anxiously, watching Caleb from the corner of his eye. Caleb was quiet for a moment, seeming to reflect inward, before shaking his head.

"No, I don't feel her." Caleb put his foot down harder on the gas pedal.

When they got to her house, Jace was out of the car before it had come to a full stop. Her door was locked, but it wasn't a match for his strength, especially in his agitated state. The handle gave under the pressure of his hand, and the door swung open.

"Sara!" Jace called out, rushing into the house. "Sara? Oh God, Sara! Caleb, get a cloth and some water." Jace fell to his knees in the living room, where Sara was prone. Jace examined her quickly to make sure it was safe to move her.

"It looks like she might have had a seizure," Jace concluded after examining Sara. She had vomited and soiled herself. "I never considered what the strain of being separated would do to her. God, how could I have been so stupid?"

Caleb clasped him on the shoulder in a show of support. "There was no way we could have known this would happen."

"I should have realized with how difficult it's been for the two of us how hard it would be for Sara. And even worse, she's been alone. At least we've had each other."

Jace lifted Sara and gently placed her on the couch, then took the damp cloth and bathed her neck and forehead. Caleb went in search of fresh clothing, and Jace quickly changed Sara's dirty clothing for the clean items Caleb brought him.

"Come on, Sara." Jace tended to her while Caleb cleaned up the mess Sara had made. "Come on, sweetheart. That's it." Jace couldn't contain the relief he felt when she began coming around.

THE PAIN THAT had racked Sara's body was gone, but in its wake, she felt bruised and tenderized. She tried to sit up, but Jace reached out to keep her from moving too quickly. Caleb came and held her hand. With both of them touching her, Sara settled in a way she hadn't felt while she was away from them.

She missed their touch, the taste of their kisses, and now that she had them back together again, it became painfully obvious how wrong it felt to be without them.

"What happened?" She accepted the glass of water Caleb passed her and let the cool liquid soothe her parched throat. Instinctively she knew it was her separation from Caleb and Jace that had caused her pain and distress.

Jace and Caleb sat with her on the sofa. "Honey, I'm so sorry. If we had known that our separation would affect you the way it has, we never would have stayed away. We never meant to hurt you with our ignorance," Jace said.

"I'm feeling better now." Sara leaned back against the cushions, letting them take her weight. The closer she was to Jace and Caleb, the better she felt. She didn't want to seem needy but couldn't tear herself away. She ran her hands over each of them, ignoring the way they trembled.

"I'm sorry," she whispered, trying to curl her fingers into a fist.

"Don't be sorry. Take what you need." Caleb unfurled her fingers and pressed her hand to his chest. "Touch us. We need it too."

Sara looked to Jace for his approval, and at his nod she shifted closer to him. "Open your shirt." She smiled when Jace complied without question.

When she touched his bare skin, electricity arced between them. When she made contact with Caleb, the heat exploded. She nuzzled against Jace's neck, burying her nose in the hollow of his throat and letting his scent wrap around her.

"Take me home."

Chapter Twenty-Four

The ride back to town passed in a blur for Caleb. He couldn't believe the difference that having Sara back made. He and Jace had been on edge the entire time she was gone, and he hadn't even realized it. It was only the absence of tension now that tipped him off to the fact that anything was different.

He cursed himself for his lack of attention to detail, berating himself for not knowing what Jace needed. It was the reason he'd never rise to full power. Being alpha of the pack meant you had to be aware of all the pack members under you. He'd never wanted the responsibility on a large scale, but now that he realized how deeply Jace had been hurting, he wished he'd been more aware.

"Stop." Jace raised his eyes to the review mirror, holding Caleb's gaze for a moment before turning his attention back to driving. "I can hear every self-doubt, and you need to stop. We have her back. We're going home. Everything is going to be fine now."

Caleb stroked her hair where she slept against his side. It was as if the internal battle had taken too much out of her, exhausting her. He'd tried to lay her flat in an attempt to make her more comfortable, but every time there was too much space between them, she panicked.

"Something is wrong." He sent the thought to Jace on their own private channel, unable to keep what he felt to himself. He almost wished that he'd reconsidered when Jace's fear permeated the car.

"I want her seen by a doctor as soon as we're back." The demand was clear in Jace's tone, and Caleb wouldn't have been able to ignore it even if he'd wanted to. Sara let out a whimper, and Jace hit the gas.

As soon as they were home, Caleb called for the doctor, hoping to put Jace at ease.

* * * *

Jace looked at the closed door before pacing again. He wanted to go in and demand answers, but the doctor—a member of the pack—had ordered him out. Fear and concern for Sara's well-being kept him there. Finally, after what seemed like an eternity, the door eased open.

"Is she okay?" Both men jumped on the doctor as soon as he exited the bedroom.

The doctor held up his hand, motioning for quiet. "She may not have our hearing, but she needs her rest. You two need to keep it down."

"Is she okay?" Jace demanded again, this time keeping his volume low while barely resisting the urge to grab the doctor by the back of his neck and shake him.

"This is new to us, Jace. She's the first human to mate with our kind that we know of. She's strong, but her body has been through tremendous stress." The doctor's gaze darted away, and Jace couldn't contain himself any longer. His hand shot out, grabbing the doctor's arm.

"What aren't you telling us? What's wrong with Sara?"

"She's pregnant."

His knees threatened to buckle, and he remained on his feet by sheer will alone. "What?"

"We didn't know it was possible. We hadn't even considered the possibility."

Jace ran his hand through his hair, tugging on the short strands. "How? Do you think the Yellow-Claw Pack knows? Does she know?" His mind was reeling with questions he wasn't sure the doctor could answer.

The doctor gave a quick shake of his head. "She does now, but she didn't have a clue before I told her. It isn't likely the Yellow-Claw Pack knew, or they wouldn't have released her when they did. I only ran a blood test to check, and I nearly had to sedate her for that. Her kidnappers really did some damage there. The poor thing was terrified as soon as I brought out the needle, but because she's showing signs similar to our women when they are breeding, I needed blood to run some additional testing. It's possible she hadn't had many human symptoms yet. She wouldn't have been able to keep something like this from you if she'd known the truth. You would sense something from her."

"How far along is she?" Caleb asked.

"As near as I can figure without a complete exam, a month. Two at the most."

"Two months. Wouldn't that mean she'd missed her cycle?"

"Again, this is all new. We have no way to know all of the unique ways our species will interact when we mate. You also have to remember she was taken and held against her will. There is a chance she missed her cycle and didn't even realize it." The doctor gave them both stern looks. "No more separation. Her body isn't handling it well, and it could cause her to miscarry or worse."

Jace felt the blood drain from his face and his lips go numb at the doctor's warning. She was quickly becoming both their greatest strength and their biggest weakness, and he couldn't imagine anything taking her from them. He'd rip his beating heart from his chest before allowing that.

"Thank you, doctor. There's not worry of that," Caleb hastened to reassure the doctor while he collected his bag and made his way to the door.

"Tell the alpha you need time with your mate. Despite what's going on within the pack, she must be your top priority."

Caleb shut the door before the doctor could say more, but they both felt chastised for allowing their mate to come to any harm.

* * * *

When Sara woke, she was surrounded by their warmth with their hands resting on her midsection, idly stroking her exposed flesh. Jace was asleep, but his thumb still traced distracting circles around her navel as if even in sleep he couldn't bear to stop touching her, and she wondered if he was dreaming.

Caleb was watching her, his gaze tracking her every movement. They lay silently watching each other as if trying to see inside the other person.

"Have you decided to stay?"

The question seemed to float out of the darkness and wrap around her. It was as clear as it would have been if Caleb had spoken the words.

Sara nodded slowly, and Caleb's arms tightened around her. It was an odd feeling, bonding with one lover while the other lay sleeping on the other side of her. It evoked feelings of turmoil within her, and not knowing what to do about it, there was no way she could keep her anxiety from rising.

Jace shifted in his sleep, drawing her closer, but the move that was meant to comfort only made her panic more. Her heart started pounding, and the arms that had been warm and inviting now felt like a trap confining her to the bed.

"Let me up. Let me up!" She pushed frantically at their arms, blinking wildly when Caleb switched on the bedside lamp, throwing the room into bright light. Jace was awake now as well and peering at her cautiously, sleep still clouding his gaze.

"What's wrong?"

"I can't breathe. Let me up." Sara kicked back the covers. Both men had removed their arms from around her waist, but she was still in between them and the large bed was suddenly too small for the three of them. Sara scrambled to the end of the bed and threw herself off, making a mad dash for the bathroom.

The room was hot and spinning, and her vision narrowed, becoming black and fuzzy around the edges. Sara feared she would pass out before she made it to the bathroom. She lurched forward in that direction, shuffling her weight against the wall.

She landed heavily against the bathroom counter and heard the men both curse from the other room. She twisted the tap, and cold water thundered out, drowning the throbbing in her ears.

Goose flesh rose on her skin when she shoved her wrists under the stream and held them there until they felt numb. Both Caleb and Jace were in the bathroom now, but she ignored them. Cupping her hands to collect the water, she lowered her head to drink.

"Are you all right now?"

"Yes. No. I don't know." She shook her head, feeling lost.

"What happened?" Jace asked gently.

"I don't know how to do this." She covered her face with her hands, too embarrassed to look at either of them.

"Know how to do what?" Caleb asked, tugging on her arms so she couldn't hide from them. She gave up resisting and allowed him to draw her hands away from her face, but she refused to meet their gaze.

"I don't know how to be with you both. So much has changed so fast. It's too much. I don't even feel like my body is my own anymore."

Caleb urged her to sit down on the toilet, crouching in front of her so they were eye to eye. "You don't have to do anything, Sara. You don't have to be anything. Just be you. Just be with us."

"How?" she wailed as tears started to flow. "Don't you see I don't know how? I haven't been with a lot of men, and now you want me to be with two—and not just any two but ones who are fierce and dominant and make me worry that I'll lose sight of myself if I'm not careful."

"If I could leave you, I would. If it would make you happy, Sara, I would. Jace mated you first. Your bond with him is already strong. I would bow out if I had the strength, but I don't, and I can't."

The thought of Caleb leaving them filled her with dread, and she felt her panic begin anew. She didn't want him to leave. She wanted him to love her. She needed him. She needed both of them, but it was a vicious cycle of confusion because not being able to understand or control the need fed her fear.

Chapter Twenty-Five

Jace wanted to talk to her about the baby, but her words rang loud in his head. *Too much too fast.* He was anxious about how their conversation would go. She was already expecting his child. He could smell the scent of his own DNA in their baby, and he was thrilled, but how did she feel? They'd had such a whirlwind courtship, there hadn't been time to discuss whether or not they wanted a family. In all honesty, he hadn't even considered if it would be possible with her being human. He couldn't sense anything from her other than exhaustion, confusion, and fear.

They would have to monitor her condition closely. It was possible that Sara and the baby could be at great risk. He didn't want to tell her how fragile this pregnancy could be, but there could be no secrets between mates. Their connection was too deep, but she would need to be told delicately.

"Just give yourself some time, Sara. You don't have to be anything but what you are. You just have to be you." Jace wet a cloth and put it along the back of her neck. "Come back to bed and get some rest. Our separation made you ill."

"Nate came to see me," she whispered when Jace had settled her in the bed again, this time giving her his side so that she would feel less overwhelmed. "He's coming to the area. Some crazy article about Bigfoot. He's coming here. If he catches even a whiff of lycans, he'll try to destroy you all."

"Shh. It's all right. He won't hurt you ever again."

"It's not me I'm worried about," she said, snuggling deeper into the covers. "He's ruthless when he gets something in his head. You have to protect yourselves. You have to protect the pack."

"Ryan can worry about the pack. He's alpha. They're his responsibility. You're our responsibility. We're concerned with your well-being. You are all that matters."

She shivered, and Jace pulled the blankets around her.

"I just can't seem to keep warm."

"That's why we put you in the middle, babe." Caleb draped his arm across Jace's hip to touch Sara as she burrowed deeper into the covers.

Jace listened as her breathing evened out again as she settled back into sleep. It was the fetus that was wreaking havoc with her body. Female lycans had difficulty regulating their temperature when expecting, but their temperatures also ran hotter. He sighed. Placing his hand over Caleb's, he allowed sleep to claim him again.

* * * *

The next morning Jace and Caleb made Sara a big breakfast, knowing she would need to eat well to keep her strength up. She appeared weary and rumpled when she joined them in the kitchen.

"Sit. Eat." Caleb pulled out her chair, and Jace put a plate in front of her.

She groaned and pushed it away.

"Eat." He placed the plate back in front of her.

"I'm not hungry. I actually feel nauseated."

Jace felt a pang of sympathy for her as he watched her complexion turn a peaked green. "You need to try to eat something." Jace moved the plate away from her again, and Caleb brought her some fruit.

"Try this instead. It might be easier on your stomach." Caleb peeled a banana and handed it to her, his worried gaze meeting Jace's above where she was seated.

"Why hasn't she said anything about the doctor about the baby or about being home? Something isn't right here." Caleb's questions were careful, but Jace felt the underlying confusion behind them.

Jace knew Caleb was right when he touched Sara's mind and felt nothing relating to the doctor's visit or the baby. Knowing that she didn't have the necessary experience to compartmentalize her memories and emotions, he suspected that she'd blocked out the visit.

"Sara, we had the doctor here. Do you remember? You were pretty out of it." Her confusion remained, and he could see the wheels spinning in her mind as she tried to piece together her memories.

She let out a low, frustrated sigh before answering. "No, I don't remember anything after leaving my house." She bit into a piece of toast that Caleb pushed toward her.

Jace watched as she chewed and swallowed before speaking again. "You don't remember anything about seeing the doctor last night?"

"No. I remember you coming to my apartment last night. I remember you putting me in the truck, and I remember waking up last night panicked and then waking up again this morning."

Jace cursed under his breath. "Our mating has confused the pack. No one is sure exactly how our species will interact especially with mating. It wasn't thought that all aspects of mating would be possible."

"Aspects of mating?"

"The doctor believes you are pregnant. He told you this when he examined you last night," Jace said.

SHOCK TORE THROUGH Sara. She couldn't be pregnant; she would have missed her period. She froze as it dawned on her that she *had* missed her last period. In the stress of being taken by the Yellow-Claw Pack and then the strain of her separation from Jace and Caleb, she hadn't realized that she was late.

"Is that why they kept taking my blood?" She shivered, remembering how weak and vulnerable they had made her feel.

"I don't think that's what they were looking for specifically," Jace reassured her. "They wanted to understand how you're different, why you're able to mate with us."

"They treated me like a goddamn lab rat," Sara spat angrily. She placed a protective hand over her stomach. "Don't tell anyone. I don't want anyone to know."

"Sara—"

"No! That other pack was horrible to me, and your pack hasn't done anything to make me feel like I'm part of your community. If I really am pregnant, I don't want anyone to know. God only knows what they would do to me if they knew." Sara pushed her plate away, no longer hungry, the toast she'd bitten into drying in her throat.

"Okay. We won't tell them, Sara. They don't have to know yet," Jace said, and Caleb nodded his agreement. "We won't tell anyone until you're ready for them to know."

Sara let out a sigh, feeling a measure of calm now that she had control over something again. "I'd like to talk to this doctor of yours again too. I have questions I need answers for."

Sara paced while she worked up the nerve to call the doctor. She'd demanded answers, but now she was afraid to go after them. Her fingers shook as she dialed the number Caleb had written down for her.

"You're sure I'm pregnant?" Sara asked almost as soon as the doctor answered. She glanced warily at the closed bedroom door, certain that Jace and Caleb would come rushing in. They'd offered to stay with her as she made the call, but it had felt important to do this on her own.

"Yes. I've examined your blood further and believe that you may have recessive lycan genes. It could be possible that one of your great ancestors was a shifter. That would explain how this was able to happen with relative ease, when for all intents and purposes, mating between the two species should present numerous challenges. There are just so many things about your mating and subsequently this pregnancy that we don't understand. It will be important to study you and monitor things closely to see how both you and the baby progress."

"I'm not a science experiment!"

"No, of course not, but you could be the first human-lycan hybrid. Think of the child you're carrying and how much easier things will be if we gain the knowledge we need now."

"You really think I could be part lycan?" She tried to ignore the tremor in her voice, unsure whether it was from excitement or fear.

"It may not be likely, but it is possible. From what I can tell, it may only be a distant relative. We can do more research once you're feeling stronger, but for now I'd recommend rest whenever you feel it necessary. Try not to overexert yourself." The doctor gave her a few more instructions before hanging up.

Sara flopped back across the bed as the reality of how much her situation had changed started to finally sink in.

"Ostara is coming in less than six weeks. It's the biggest of our celebrations. It's the event that brings the pack together and cements us as a unit. The burned buildings have begun to be rebuilt. Things have quieted down with the Yellow-Claw Pack, at least for now. This year's celebration will be more extravagant than anything we do the rest of the year. You need to be there. It's important that you take your proper place within the pack."

"Why does it even matter to you? You didn't even want to come back here. You'd left the pack, so why does it matter if I claim anything at all? I'm not a lycan. I'm not like you." Sara could feel anger bubbling up within her. She suspected that her outburst was due, at least in part, to her hormones, but she was unable to rein her emotions in. They'd seemed elated when she told them the doctor's theory about her having shifter DNA.

"You behaved in such an elemental way when we were at the ritual clearing, it wouldn't surprise me at all if the doctor was right."

Their excitement made her resentful; it made her feel as if her being fully human wasn't good enough for them.

"Maybe we all need a bit of a break from talk of babies, the pack, and being a shifter. Let's go out today. We can enjoy each other's company and take pictures by the lake," Caleb suggested.

"We can't just sweep our problems under the rug and expect that they'll go away," she snapped at him, anger making her words sharp.

"I'm not saying we should ignore our problems. Just that maybe we need a bit of a break to gain perspective. I'd like to spend time together doing something you enjoy. I'd like to do something that makes us all happy."

Sara perked up at that. The nature magazine she'd submitted her pictures to had asked to see more and for her to submit a sample piece for their upcoming spring issue. She was itching to get outside behind the lens and capture the world as it woke to spring.

* * * *

There was still snow on the ground, but it had softened, and it squelched under their feet as they moved through the woods toward the lake. The men were patient, silently watching as she waited to catch the right shots, the sun streaming through the trees glinting off the snow on the ground, water droplets hanging off hidden leaves. She tried to capture things that had been untouched.

"The magazine really wanted something different. I had been hoping to get some wildlife shots."

"I think we can help with that," Caleb said, looking to Jace for confirmation. At Jace's nod, Caleb began stripping out of his clothes. Sara watched the change flow through him.

One moment he was a man standing before her, and the next minute he was a dark0gray wolf standing on all four paws. He stamped his front paws in the snow, shaking his big body.

"We'll scare up some game for you to photograph," Jace encouraged.

"Are you sure? What if I catch one of you on camera?"

"There are differences if you know what you're looking for, but for something like this, even if you did catch us on camera accidentally, you don't have to submit those pictures for the magazine. It should be fine."

Sara needed no further urging. She raised the camera and became lost in the world of her photos, laughing as the men had rabbits running her way.

After she'd taken several pictures, Sara found herself smiling, her earlier anger put aside. Their play reminded her of the dreams she'd had of the three of them.

Moving toward them, she gave in to the urge to bury her hands in their fur, then stroked their heads in turn.

"May I take a picture of you? One of the three of us together?" she asked, petting along Caleb's spine. "Just for me to keep." Jace nodded, and Sara squeezed between them, taking a couple of pictures of the three of them. She laughed when Caleb licked the side of her face.

"Yuck!" Sara wiped the moisture from her cheek, giggling when Jace nudged her side.

Chapter Twenty-Six

When they returned to the house, Jace and Caleb realized they were in trouble. The majority of the pack was meeting behind their backs, and Jace wanted to tear them all apart. He gnashed his teeth together.

"Wait here," Jace barked, and he stalked toward the town hall where the pack was meeting.

"What's going on? Jace?" Sara called Jace back, determined to go after him.

"Sara, wait." Caleb went after her, but she burst through the door on Jace's heels.

"She's human. It isn't right," a woman in the third row yelled out. "They were in the woods, and she was taking pictures of them as wolves. Why would she do that, if not to expose us and bring harm to the pack?"

Jace growled, unable to hold back his anger. "Why not ask instead of holding this meeting behind our backs?" He watched Sara's face crumple in defeat as she accepted the fact that many of the pack saw her as different and believed she'd never belong.

He shot daggers at his brother for having allowed the meeting and cursed that he wasn't alpha. If pack rules hadn't dictated that, to win the position of alpha, he might have to kill Ryan, he could be alpha now and none of this would be happening. If that were the case, though, it would be unlikely that he ever would have met Sara, and he wouldn't wish that away.

"Sara, go home with Caleb." He watched her shoulders tense as she tried to hold her emotions together, to be strong in front of the pack, and he admired her for it, but he had no desire to subject her to more of their cruelty.

She shook her head. "I'll go. If they really don't want me here, I'll go." She moved to leave, and Jace caught her by the waist.

"No. You're not leaving. Not because they want you to. If you leave, it will because you want to leave, because you don't love us, because we aren't your true mates. They can't force us apart, and they know that." He squeezed her in a hug, sending reassuring vibes along the path of their shared communication, encouraging her to think of the baby she carried and consider them as a family unit, rather than to think of them each individually. He kissed her forehead before handing her to Caleb.

"Take her home. I'll deal with this." He sneered in the direction of the pack.

Jace waited until Caleb had led her out of the door and was sure they were out of earshot before turning on the pack again.

"How dare you!"

"Just a second." Ryan tried to step in and assert his dominance.

"No! She's my mate! Not just some woman I'm seeing—she's my mate! You should be ashamed of yourselves. We can't control who our mates are. You know that! Too many of you have forgotten what it means to truly mate."

"The pack has a right to be concerned."

"No, Ryan, they don't. They're concerned because she's human? What a bunch of intolerant, bigoted assholes!"

"Our number-one concern has to be to protect the pack. You know that."

"This is such bullshit. You all but ordered me back here. I would have been perfectly content to keep my mate away from the pack!"

* * * *

When Caleb brought Sara back to the house, she expected that he wouldn't leave her, but he told her he had to go back to help Jace. She wasn't surprised, though. Even as far away from him as she was, she could still feel the anger inside him. She was glad that Caleb would help keep him from doing something reckless or stupid.

Sara rubbed her palm over her abdomen. It was flat; there was no external sign that she was pregnant. She felt weaker at times, dizzy and disoriented in the morning, but that could still be from the ordeal she'd suffered.

The house suddenly felt confining as she lay there trying to process everything. She lived with two men in an interspecies ménage relationship surrounded by a community of people who thought she was inferior to them.

It made her feel dejected, and the walls felt like they were closing in on her. Before panic could overtake her, she threw on her shoes and slipped out of the house. She didn't plan to go far. She just needed to be out in the open to clear her head.

She sat down on a boulder at the edge of a field, huddling down inside her coat. She didn't know how long she sat there lost to her own thoughts, but when the sun started sinking in the sky, the air became damp and chilled.

When the familiar scent of smoke in the air teased her nostrils, fear spread through her. The majority of the pack was at that awful meeting, discussing whether or not she was good enough for them, while more of the town burned.

She ran toward the smoke and the squeal of frightened animals, realizing quickly that it wasn't the sound of trapped, livestock she was hearing but children.

Turning in the direction of the sound, she pushed herself harder, not certain she would get there in time but knowing she had to try. What she found on the other side of the field made her blood run cold. They had been trapped in the barn on purpose.

Sara clawed at the boards that had been nailed over the door, wishing for superhuman strength to remove them. She poured her distress and anguish into a thought for Jace and Caleb, uncertain if they would understand or even get her message.

When the left side of the board budged, Sara used all her adrenaline to kick the door. Pain shot up her leg, but three solid kicks later, she was inside.

Smoke billowed out of the opening, making Sara's lungs burn. She pulled her shirt up to cover her nose and mouth before stepping into the barn. A small figure knocked past her, causing her to lose her balance. Another clung to her, and she pried the girl off, pointing her to the direction of the opening.

Tear streamed from her eyes, making it harder to see, but she could just barely tell there were three forms huddled together. She crept toward them slowly, trying to keep low to the ground where the air was clearer.

She pushed them to safety, intending to follow them out, but she didn't see the low-hanging beam through the haze and hit her head.

* * * *

By the time they reached the barn, the back half was burning steadily. Five of the pack's children clutched each other, sobbing. Guilt that the anger he'd been feeling toward his brother and the pack had kept him from hearing Sara clearly swamped Jace, making it hard to breathe. If he had heard her, they would have been able to reach the barn sooner.

"It's too late for the livestock, but at least the children got out." Jace scanned the small crowd, looking for Sara.

"Should we let it burn? It's not close enough to other buildings to spread."

"Fine."

There was a tug on Jace's pant leg. He bent down and scooped up Robyn. The little girl was six years old and covered in soot and dirt from the fire. "Everything is going to be okay now, sweetie."

"Who's going to get Sara? Someone has to go get her. I didn't see her come out."

"What?" His gaze darted to the burning barn and back to the little girl, who was watching with just as much horror in her eyes. Jace looked over the crowd again, desperately searching for Sara and feeling more frantic when he couldn't find her.

Without thinking, Jace set Robyn down and ran to the door of the barn. "SARA!" When she didn't answer, he threw himself blindly through the opening. Even with his superior eyesight, making things out was nearly impossible.

He stumbled forward, almost falling over her prone form when he finally found her. The whole process took him less than three minutes, but it felt like a lifetime.

When they exited, he laid her out on the grass a safe distance from the barn. She was still, and with the other sounds surrounding them, he couldn't make out her heartbeat.

"What did you do, Sara? Oh God, what did you do?" He lay his head against her chest, listening for her heart as he searched for her pulse.

When he heard the faint thump, he wanted to whoop with joy. "She needs oxygen. We need to get her to a hospital."

"Jace, we can't risk that your mating would have changed her in any way that the doctors would be able to detect."

"No! She's pregnant, Ryan. I won't risk her life or the life of our baby."

Ryan's mouth dropped open. "What the hell was she doing running into a burning building if she's pregnant? Why wouldn't she wait for help instead of foolishly putting herself at risk?"

Jace was shocked when Caleb let his fist fly. It smashed into Ryan's face with a loud crack. "There were children in that barn. You continue to think she's less than us because she's human. Did you stop to consider that she did it because there wasn't time to wait for us? She thought only of saving the children and not about her own safety. No one in this pack has lifted a finger to befriend her, but she still rushed into danger to help others. Does that earn her the spot within our pack that should have been hers to begin with the moment we mated? Ostara is only five weeks away, the biggest holiday that unifies the pack, and all anyone has done is make her feel unwelcome."

Ryan glared at Caleb while rubbing his jaw. "You get that one because you're worried about her, but don't forget your place."

Jace's claws came out at Ryan's threat. "We don't have time for this. Either help me get her to a hospital or figure out a way for me to help her."

Chapter Twenty-Seven

They didn't take her to the hospital. What they did was get her to the town's doctor and put her on oxygen. When she finally started to come around, Jace breathed a sigh of relief.

"Sara, don't try to move. No, no, keep the mask on," he said, gently swatting her hands away from the oxygen mask as she tried to pull it off. "Leave it on."

"Did they get out?" she asked, her voice muffled behind the oxygen mask.

"Yes, they got out. Everyone is fine, though you very nearly were not. You need to rest, and you need the oxygen. Your lungs took in a lot of smoke."

Jace had never been so grateful for his training as a paramedic. He hated Ryan for not allowing him to take her to the hospital, but he was encouraged that she'd gained more color in her cheeks.

"You're not to move from this bed for at least the next forty-eight hours. Not until I'm sure that you and my baby are all right."

SARA WINCED AS guilt stabbed through her. She hadn't even considered her own health or the fetus she was carrying. She still didn't feel any different, but that was no excuse for being reckless. Though she had no regrets over saving the children, she was horrified that she hadn't even considered the well-being of her own child.

"How do you know it's yours?" Her voice was muffled again, and it frustrated her. She longed to pull the plastic away from her face, but she feared that if she did, Jace would stop talking and would make her go to sleep.

"Scent."

"What?"

"When I'm close to your skin, especially the skin of your lower abdomen, I can smell the baby. The scent is familial. The baby shares my DNA."

The idea that Jace could smell the baby, that he could tell that much about it even this early on, fascinated her and made her wonder if there was a limit to what his kind could do. It also had her questioning what her child would be capable of and whether or not she could be an adequate parent to someone with skills she could only dream of.

"Can you tell the sex?"

"No. It's far too early for that, and even if it weren't, gender isn't something that can be scented."

"If it had belonged to Caleb, would you have been upset?" She watched him carefully for his answer.

"No. You're ours, and the baby is too. It doesn't matter who the biological father is. We are a family."

"If the baby is human, will they fit into the pack?" she asked, already feeling a parental need to protect her child.

"We'll make sure they do," Jace said with so much conviction that it was hard to believe anything else was a possibility.

"What if I'm a horrible mother? I'm not a shifter. What if I can never be what our child needs?"

"I know you're afraid, but every parent worries about being a good parent, don't they?"

She nodded. "It's more than that, though. I'm human. If the baby is lycan, like you, can I really parent a child who will have abilities that I can't even fathom?"

"Will you love our child, Sara?"

"Of course! I feel like I already do." She moved to pull the mask away from her face, but Jace stopped her.

"All our child needs is your love. There's nothing greater or more powerful in this world. It won't matter to them if you're human or a lycan."

Sara realized he was right—she would love their child with all her heart, and being human wouldn't change the love she felt at all.

* * * *

A sense of déjà vu rattled Jace as Ryan called the meeting to order. The remaining council members were all in attendance, and Jace fully expected that they would object to Sara being part of the pack and their mating, but also in the crowd were the parents of the children Sara had saved. For the first time, Jace felt a sense of hope.

"I don't even know why we're still debating this," Kelly, the highest-ranked female in the pack, spoke up.

Without an official alpha female, the women of Coldridge looked to her on many of the important decisions and dynamics of how the women conducted themselves. Despite her being in her twenties, most of the older women were willing to defer to her judgement as well.

If it hadn't been for the fact that Ryan drove her crazy and that she was several years younger than they were, Jace suspected she would have made an excellent mate for his brother.

"We're debating this, Kelly, because she's human and her children will be human!" The council member representing the Clear Creek pack snapped at her, and Ryan growled a warning until the council member backed down.

"You can't control mating. You have two choices. Either she stays as a full member of the pack, or the three of us leave," Jace said.

"She saved our children. She's not a threat," one of the parents spoke loudly from the front row.

It made Jace proud that there were members of his pack willing to support his mate, despite their differences.

"We have so few children these days. We would be foolish to dilute our bloodlines with the inferior blood of humans," the council member for the Flat Plains pack spoke.

"We can't be afraid of change. The addition of new genetics could be just the thing that helps save our pack!"

"It's possible any children produced from the union will be fully human. We have to prepare for that possibility," the same council member spoke again.

"Would that really be so horrible?" Caleb asked.

"I think it's time to change things up. There are open seats on the council. The pack should hold nominations for the spots," one of the other parents suggested.

A cheer went through the pack.

They were clearly ready for change, hungry for it, and Jace saw his moment to make a real difference to the dynamics of all the packs.

"I'd like to be considered." He threw his name into the ring, and another round of cheers rang out through the crowd. A few other challengers submitted their names as well, and it could no longer be denied that the new council seats would be filled not with handpicked nominees but with new members who'd proven themselves powerful enough to hold the reins.

"We'll hold the trials and nominations at the Ostara celebration."

It wouldn't leave Jace much time to prepare, and he knew that was why the council had set it up that way. They were afraid. He couldn't smell it—they hid it better than that—but he caught a glint of it from time to time in the way they looked at him. His power scared them.

* * * *

"Five weeks to prepare? Jace, that's crazy! You need more time." Caleb poured them both a drink. "It's going to be a tremendous strain for you to do this."

"Is it dangerous?"

They both turned toward Sara at the sound of her voice.

"I don't want you to do anything dangerous." Her voice quivered, and Caleb went to her and wrapped his arm around her, offering her the comfort she needed.

"It will be all right." He kissed her temple, brushing her hair back from her face to meet her eyes.

"You just said it would be stressful for him. You don't have to lie to me. They already treat me differently, and I don't need the two of you acting like I'm less than you. Like I'm just some…thing to coddle."

"You are not a thing for us to coddle. You're our mate, and you are ours to take care of, but we'll never lie to you."

"You may not lie outright, but you hold things back that you don't think I can handle, and it drives me crazy."

"We never meant to keep things from you. As our mate, our first thought is always to protect you."

"Keeping me in the dark isn't protecting me. It's doing what's easiest for you when it's too hard or too uncomfortable to explain something to me, and it makes me feel like a kept pet. Not someone you love or respect."

"You're right, and we're sorry. From now on we'll try not to withhold things from you. The challenge will be a strain, but I am extremely powerful. They've underestimated me. It won't be something I can't handle." Jace kissed her, enfolding both of them in his embrace.

Sara let out a sigh, and her contentment was almost palpable to Caleb.

"All we want to do is keep you safe, Sara. Keep you and our family safe and together. If Jace does this, they won't be able to separate us."

If it didn't work, they would have to leave the pack, because they would never let her go. They would never give each other up. Their bond was growing and would continue to do so once they completed their joining during the Ostara celebration. They would declare themselves to each other in front of the entire pack under the glow of the moon, where they would again inflict the mating bond wounds on one another. Their connection would vibrate though the pack, adding to its harmony. It would also mean a deeper joining with the pack, as the communication that Jace and Caleb shared with the pack would extend to her as well. She would sense the echo of the group's emotions and well-being as they would sense hers. The pack would have to accept the three of them as a unit before the joining.

Chapter Twenty-Eight

Five weeks passed by in the blink of an eye, and as she watched Jace prepare for what he would face to become part of the council, Sara could only wish that he had more time.

He set a grueling pace for himself, pushing his limits and testing his stamina. It was difficult for Sara to watch, and when he came home each night after putting in a long day, she couldn't help but wonder if it was all worth it.

She was waiting for Jace and Caleb to come home, still uncomfortable with being alone for long periods of time. When someone knocked on the door, she tensed, uncertain whether or not she should open the door.

"Sara, are you home? It's Kelly. I've brought you some lunch."

Sara wished that she had the senses of a wolf, but despite the fact that she'd begun to feel different in the last week, she wasn't sure if it meant her senses were changing or even if the way she was feeling was a good thing.

"I'll just leave it for you if you'd like," Kelly spoke through the door.

"No, no." Sara pulled open the door. "Please come in."

Kelly was holding a casserole dish. "I've brought you some beef stew. I wanted to say thank you for what you did for my family. My niece was one of the children you rescued. I know it's not much, but I wanted to show my appreciation. I hope you like the stew."

Sara's stomach rumbled at the mention of food, and she blushed, embarrassed. "Sorry. It seems like I'm always hungry these days."

"That's natural. My sister ate just about anything that wasn't nailed down when she was expecting. It might be an indication that the baby will be lycan. How are you feeling otherwise?" Kelly asked, putting the stew in the oven to warm.

"I didn't want to tell anyone I was pregnant. I made Jace and Caleb promise that we could wait." Anger simmered to the surface and made Sara's words bitter. She had asked them specifically not to tell anyone, and they had told her they would and then had disregard her wishes.

"Don't be mad at the guys, please. I didn't come here to cause trouble."

"I can't help it! They promised me." A profound sense of sadness claimed Sara, and she struggled to pull herself together.

"Jace told Ryan that you were pregnant, not because he was intentionally betraying your trust but because he needed to get you medical attention as quickly as possible. I know we weren't really friendly when you first got here with Caleb and Jace. I wish that I could go back and change that, but I'd like to be your friend now if you'd let me."

"Do you have a mate?" Sara asked, anxious to talk to another woman who had experienced what she was going through.

"No." Sadness crept into Kelly's voice, and it made Sara want to reach out to her. "I thought for a time that there was a mate within the pack for me, but it doesn't seem like that's the case. You really can talk to me, though. You don't have to hide what you're feeling."

Sara gave a nervous laugh. "You can probably tell anyway, right? That's part of this whole superior lycan thing?"

Kelly shook her head, and her face crumpled. It didn't take being able to sense emotions to know she'd hurt the woman.

"I'm sorry. I guess my defenses are still up. I'm feeling okay, I guess. I don't really know what's normal. I've never been pregnant before, let alone pregnant with a baby whose father is a lycan."

"I'm sorry we've been so terrible to you. I never stopped to consider how strange and difficult things must be for you."

Sara placed her hand on her stomach, a protective gesture she couldn't seem to stop. Over the past few days, her pregnancy bump seemed to have become more pronounced—a testament to the fact that her baby had more than human DNA as she expanded quicker than normal. Sara hid her thickening waistline with baggy clothing, and only her mates and the doctor were aware of her increased growth. The rest of the pack hadn't noticed the difference yet. She was sure if they had, she'd be subjected to scrutiny. Jace and Caleb would worry about her and might even be forced to defend her. She didn't want to put them into that situation again. There had been enough stress and worry since she'd been with them.

"There is just so much that I don't understand. I wish more was known about why few lycan females are born and what that will mean for my baby."

"I'm sure there won't be anything wrong with your baby. You should be excited, especially with Ostara coming up. Your baby is cause for even greater happiness."

"Kelly, everyone keeps talking about the Ostara celebration. What goes on at the celebration?"

"It's a time of rebirth when the pack reconnects with the earth and each other. This year will be an even bigger celebration. This year Ostara coincides with a super moon, and although lycans aren't dependent on the moon to change form, the pull of a moon like this is undeniable."

"Will the entire pack change? Will I be the only human?" Sara was nervous about being the only human among wolves. At the Imbolc bonfire, there had been both wolves and humans, some of the pack choosing to remain in their human forms, so she hadn't felt overwhelmed or alone, but if what Kelly said was true and the whole pack felt compelled to change, she might be the only human.

"No one will hurt you, Sara. You don't have to be afraid." Kelly pulled the stew from the oven and served Sara a bowl. "I know we weren't very warm, but honestly, after how you saved our kids, no one would dare hurt you. It was so brave."

"It didn't feel brave. I just had to help. Are the kids okay?"

"They've recovered," Kelly said, cutting a slice of bread for Sara. She was putting it on the table when Jace came through the door, dripping in blood.

"What the hell happened?" Sara gasped, jumping to her feet.

"Training."

"Training for what, for the love of God? You look like you've been to war," Sara said.

"I'll be fine. I just need to shower." He shrugged off her hand, and Sara tried not to feel hurt by the rejection, but the fact that they had company made it so much worse. It stung her pride that he'd treat her that way in front of one of the pack members and seemed to undermine not only their relationship but her fragile standing within the pack.

"I'll get out of your hair," Kelly said. "Don't take his attitude too hard. A challenge like this is hard on anyone, and five weeks isn't a lot of time to prepare. Thanks again for what you did for my family." Kelly squeezed her hand in a show of support, but Sara still felt the rejection keenly.

Once Kelly left, Sara wanted to go to Jace, but she feared what his reaction would be. As the days passed and Ostara drew closer, Jace seemed to grow more distant. Caleb wasn't much better, and it was obvious that he was just as worried about how the challenge would go. They were very careful about her seeing too much of the training or what the challenge would entail once they saw how intensely she was affected. They did try to prepare her for what would happen by explaining what Jace would have to endure physical pain and mental control over both his human and animal form, but the things they explained were so beyond anything Sara could imagine.

* * * *

Sara's concerns about what was happening inside her body continued to grow. The afternoon of the Ostara celebration, the twinges she'd been feeling in her stomach and back had bloomed into pain, and she couldn't pretend any longer that something wasn't going on.

She tapped lightly on the door to their home office before poking her head inside. Jace and Caleb were bent together over the desk, deep in conversation with last-minute strategizing. They both turned to look at her.

"I'm sorry. I don't mean to interrupt, but I needed to talk to you." Her gaze darted from one man to the other before dropping to the floor in fear that she'd be unwanted.

"What is it, sweetheart?" Caleb asked.

"I know it isn't the best time for this, but I'm not feeling very well." A sharp burst of hot pain went through her, making her clutch her stomach.

"What's wrong?" Jace was at her side instantly, tipping her chin so she could no longer avoid looking directly at him.

"I'm okay. I'm just not feeling great."

JACE WATCHED AS she shuddered in pain and felt like the biggest asshole. He'd been so preoccupied with preparing for the challenge, he'd been neglecting Sara, and he hadn't wanted her to worry so he'd been shielding her against his thoughts. He just hadn't realized how strongly.

"Sara, I'm so sorry, honey. What's going on? How do you feel?"

"I don't really know what's going on. I'm okay, I think. I'm just really achy, and my heart is racing." She squeezed her eyes shut, forcing the tear that had gathered in her lashes to slide over her cheek.

"Come lie down." Caleb helped her to the loveseat.

"I'm sorry. I'm fine, really. I don't mean to be so dramatic. I just feel strange."

"Strange how? Could this be from the fire?" Caleb asked, his gaze darting between them while Jace took her pulse.

Jace didn't answer while he focused on counting the beats. When he was done, he slid his hand into hers, interlocking their fingers together. "Your heart rate is a little high but not something to worry about."

"Is this normal?" Sara asked, pulling up her shirt to expose the swell of her belly, which had expanded even further than the last time they'd seen her growing baby bump. The worry was obvious in her tone.

Jace smiled. "It's fine. Lycan babies are bigger than human babies, and you're petite."

Sara propped herself up on her elbows. "Are you sure?"

"We'll have the doctor take another look at you, but I don't want you to worry. There may be some differences, and this is the first time we've ever been through this, but you can be sure we'll take every precaution. It seems the baby might be here quicker than any of us had expected."

Sara gasped, and Jace realized having the baby sooner than they'd anticipated hadn't crossed her mind. "Why didn't you tell us about how you were feeling?"

Sara looked embarrassed. Wanting to know what she was thinking, Jace lowered the shields between them and realized for the first time since he'd begun training how fully he'd locked her out. The sense of rejection emanating from her broke his heart.

"Oh honey, no, I never meant to make you feel like I didn't love you or that I didn't want you. I've just been so absorbed with Ostara and the challenge that I wasn't thinking. I haven't wanted you to feel anything that I've had to go through to prepare for this."

"It's all right," she hastened to reassure him, but it wasn't okay. He needed to be better than that, needed to treat her better than he had; otherwise what he was doing to win the challenge would be for nothing.

"Rest for now. We want you at full strength for tonight so you can participate in the public claiming." He pulled the blanket from the back of the loveseat across her, helping her get comfortable.

Once she was settled, Caleb began talking about ways for Jace to best conserve his energy during the challenge. He spoke using their mental link to avoid disturbing Sara, who'd finally dropped off into a restless nap, but Jace was unable to concentrate. Every sound she made drew his gaze back to her.

Chapter Twenty-Nine

This year's celebration started earlier than normal. Jace's challenge was first, and then they would feast as a pack, enjoying the spoils of their last hunt.

"Jace will step into the stone circle, and the challenge will begin. You can't look away. As his mates, we are also judged and must show strength and a united front," Caleb explained.

Jace kissed her. "No fear, babe. It's going to be all right," he whispered against the shell of her ear as he let his hand drift over the soft swell of her stomach, claiming their child in front of the pack.

She'd wanted to wear something that would continue to hide her pregnancy, but Jace had asked her not to.

"It's important for the pack to see the evidence of our union. It's vital they see that we're already a cohesive family unit."

He'd smiled when she'd agreed, and now in front of the entire pack, he felt enormous pride at the courage she displayed. He claimed her lips a final time in a sweet, lingering kiss before turning to Caleb and bestowing the same affection upon his second mate so that neither would be viewed as more important than the other. When he stepped away, Caleb took Sara's hand and led her to the seats at the edge of the circle, from where they would watch.

Jace tore his gaze away from his mates, unable to watch the horror in Sara's eyes at what would happen next. He stripped down to his boxers and had time to take a deep breath to center himself before he was joined in the circle by the six remaining council members. Each held an item that would inflict pain. Some would fight with fist or claw. Others had a paddle, a whip, chains, and a Taser. Each would attack him in turn, and he would have to fight the urge to change. It was torture, but it would prove that he was both mentally and physically strong.

"You have challenged to join the elder's council far before your time. To be accepted, you must face three trials to prove yourself worthy. Do you accept?"

Jace nodded. "I accept." His voice carried clearly over the area where the pack had gathered.

"Then begin."

He took the first punch easily, barely rocked by the blow, but he knew worse would follow and braced himself for a second impact. The paddle came next, catching him across the buttocks and lower back. The quick burst of pain made him grit his teeth, but there would be more. He took all their blows in stride, knowing that their aim was to wear him down, yet he still felt in control of himself.

The blinding-hot pain of the Taser buckled his knees, and he could feel the power of his beast rising to the forefront of his consciousness. He remained standing by sheer strength of will as he swallowed the power down and his inner wolf snarled at him. The whip caught him across the shoulder blades, first a dull thud and then a sharp sting as more force was applied.

A warm wash of fluid signaled the splitting of his skin as blood rolled down his back in rivulets that sped up with the beating of his heart. His wolf roared again, this time at the anguish he could feel emanating from their mate rather than the pain. He didn't want to hurt Sara—it was wrong that she had to endure seeing him go through this—but he trusted Caleb to keep her safe. Jace cut off their mental link, needing to concentrate fully on the task at hand.

This was arguably the hardest part of the challenge, and he'd nearly made it through. The next round of abuse was difficult as the whip and Taser were applied at the same time, bathing his body in hot and cold pain until the lines blurred and he was unable to distinguish between the two.

When they let up, Jace was on his knees, his sides heaving. He didn't recall falling to his knees, but this portion of the challenge was over. He breathed out a sigh of relief and forced himself to his feet. If he couldn't get to his feet under his own power, he'd forfeit the challenge. He was given a small reprieve between the first challenge and the second.

"You have performed admirably. Are you ready for your next challenge?"

Jace nodded. "Yes."

"Then change."

This portion of the challenge would further test his control over his inner animal: he would have to change multiple times in rapid succession. The pain they'd subjected him to would make changing more difficult, and he blew out a breath to ready himself.

"Change."

Jace let the power required for the change flow through him. Gathering it into himself, he loosened the hold he kept on his inner wolf, letting it come forward. The change swept through him, changing him seamlessly from a human to a wolf. He held the form for a few moments before reversing the flow of power to become human again.

The first change was actually energizing. It healed his wounds and made his body feel stronger. The second was harder, the third was draining, and the fourth and fifth blended together. The sixth had sweat beading on his brow. The seventh made his sides heave, and there was little space between the eighth and ninth. With the tenth he thought he would pass out as his vision blurred narrowing to pinpoints, and Jace had to fight the urge to vomit.

He was given slightly longer between rounds this time and chanced a look around at the spectators as he recovered. There were members of the council who appeared pleased and a few who seemed angry. Several of the pack wore expressions of awe. His brother was nervous, Caleb proud, and Sara miserable.

He wanted to go to her, to offer comfort. He wanted to offer her reassurances that he was fine, but leaving the circle was not permitted until the challenge was complete, and stopping after he'd come this far was unthinkable.

Uncertain of how much time they would allow before the next challenge, Jace prepared himself. This challenge would be difficult, not because he was unable to shift individual parts of his body but because the pain and excessive shifting would make the type of control that changing specific parts of his body required incredibly difficult.

He would be required to shift his torso so that he was half man, half wolf, and then an arm, and finally a single claw.

He drew on the power that allowed him to shift. It was there, always ready to serve him, but his wolf was weary and he almost faltered. It was only the flood of love and support that he felt through his shared link with Caleb and Sara that renewed his strength.

Jace shifted his form, leaving himself with the head and chest of a wolf on the legs of a man. He held the pose until told to release it and then shifted his arm into a front paw before shifting back to human form and changing just a single claw.

A loud cheer went through the entire pack as several members rushed forward to congratulate him, but Jace ignored them, stumbling toward his mates.

They enfolded him in their arms, and while it was comforting, their touch on his overly sensitized skin was also excruciating.

"Here, drink this." Council member Ian shoved a glass into Jace's hand.

His fingers were numb, and he had to grip the glass tight to prevent dropping it on the ground.

"Go on, drink. It will help."

His arm trembled as he brought the glass to his lips. The liquid in the glass went down thick and sweet, coating his throat with its heavily medicinal taste. Almost instantly the excess sensitivity faded and the fatigue that had been plaguing him vanished. He felt re-energized and invigorated.

Chapter Thirty

Watching what Jace had to endure was horrible. Even having Caleb with her hadn't eased the pain.

"I'm fine. Sara. It's all over now."

"Really?"

"Yes, it's all over. Let's go enjoy the rest of the celebration. Come on. The hard part is done."

Jace's challenge had taken over two hours to complete. In that time, dinner had finished cooking. Sara's stomach growled as they pulled a roast suckling pig off the fire. There was also deer and a multitude of side dishes.

Everyone sat down, and they waited for Ryan to begin. Once he dug in, they ate their fill. During the meal, several of the pack members came by to congratulate Jace on completing the challenge successfully.

"What's next?" Sara whispered once they were alone again. They'd explained as much as they could about what to expect in an effort to prepare her for what the event would be like, but experiencing the celebration herself was far more different than she expected.

"Once we've finished dinner, we'll gather in the clearing for a moon blessing. The pack will reconnect with each other and with the earth. Then we will commit ourselves to each other in front of the pack like we talked about." Caleb buttered a biscuit and put it on her plate.

"Ugh. I can't eat any more. I'm stuffed." She pushed the food back at him, laughing when he bit into it with enthusiasm.

Once dinner was over, the pack filed into the clearing. The power that emanated from the pack in that sacred place was tangible. Several of the pack members began drumming, and the beat thrummed through her body and into the ground. Ryan blessed the pack, pledging the group to the moon.

"Our blood pours though each other. One circle unbroken, ruled by the moon, controlled by the tides."

Sara could feel the connection that Jace and Caleb had spoken of through the soles of her feet. She could feel the sway of the moon, and the urge to strip her clothes off and bask in the rays of light was intense. It was almost undeniable.

She threw her shields open, wanting Caleb and Jace to know what she was feeling. The desire to be close to them raced through her system, and she didn't care that the pack was there witnessing her lust. It didn't matter that they could smell her arousal and her sweat.

Her heart raced faster, and her body flushed. Sara felt as if something was alive under her skin. "My skin feels like it's going to split open. My bones are going to snap. What's going on?" The first inklings of fear crept in.

"Open your mind fully. Let us see what's going on," Jace encouraged.

Sara pushed through her last barriers.

"Sara, what you're feeling—it's exactly how a lycan feels before their first change."

Shock ripped through her system. "How is that possible? It's not, is it?" She let the men pull her close.

"It shouldn't be. You're not a lycan, even if you do have recessive genes. Our kind aren't bitten like you see in the movies. That's just fantasy, but what you're feeling is exactly what we experience before our first change. It's how things feel before each change, but we learn to recognize the signs and it gets easier when we know what to expect."

"Why is this happening? What do I do?" Fear that the baby would somehow be injured if she was able to shift held her rigid.

"It must be the baby." Jace called the doctor forward.

"Sara, you do have recessive genes, and all female shifters have to change during pregnancy. They are compelled to do so. Changing, if you're able, won't put the fetus in danger. As you change, your uterus will too. The baby will be perfectly safe."

The doctor's words took the edge of her fear away. She looked to her mates for guidance.

"When the moon breaks through the clouds, visualize yourself shifting. Picture your body forming into a wolf. Let it flow through you like water."

Sara could see the image of a wolf in her mind, similar to how she had dreamed of Jace and Caleb. "You're sure it's safe for the baby?" she asked. Now that she could picture the wolf, she wanted to try to bring her out, but she couldn't risk their child.

"Female wolves shift during pregnancy. It helps ensure that the baby will be able to shift in adulthood. Your body will shift as a whole. The baby will be safe. Just let it come." Jace fed the doctor's words back her, hoping to reinforce their truth in her mind.

The moon broke free from the clouds, and Sara stopped fighting what she was feeling. Jace and Caleb helped her strip off her clothing. Sara ignored the curious stares of the pack around her, and when the next urge hit her, she threw back her head and howled. Her voice split the air, first wholly human and then wolf, and by the time the sound died away, she was on her hands and knees in the clearing.

Only they weren't hands and knees. They were paws. Sara howled again, and this time the pack followed suit. She could hear them now in a way that was similar to how she communicated with Jace and Caleb, but it was different too, more communal.

The night came alive around her, and she took off, needing to run. To feel the night against her skin with senses that were completely new and changed from what they'd been only moments before.

The men were on her heels, allowing her to lead while still steering her away from danger. She howled again, and they gave chase. When they reached the area by the lake, Sara stopped. Realized she didn't know how to turn back and felt a moment of panic.

Jace and Caleb projected the instructions into her mind, showing her clearly what she had to do to revert back to being a human. It was as easy as thinking what she wanted.

When she stood in front of them again, they were all human and lust was coursing through her as if it were a raging river that broke through a dam.

"Is it always like this?" she panted and clenched her legs together.

Jace and Caleb chuckled. The sound was purely masculine and stoked her already primed nerve endings. "No, but it will be like this for a while."

"Oh God!" Her arousal was so thick it slid from her sex and dampened her thighs. She couldn't imagine feeling this way every time she shifted. "I need you, both of you. Now, together." They exchanged a glance, and Sara wanted to growl. "Don't make me beg." She would if that was what they needed.

They were her alphas—they were dominant to her. She would defer to them in this. Even being equal in all other things, they owned her in this.

She opened her mouth to beg, and Jace silenced her with a kiss. Curling his hand around her neck, he drew her to him, claiming her mouth in a way he'd not done before. He kept their lips fused together while he guided her to the ground. Instinctively Sara knew that this time would be rough. They would do their best not to hurt her, but their coupling would be frenzied. Rather than being frightened, the idea excited her. She whimpered when she felt his hands on her skin. She jumped when his thumbs parted her sex, spreading her open. Sara fought the urge to push back against him as cool air kissed her flesh.

Just as she was about to open her mouth and beg him to do something, his tongue swiped though the copious fluid of her arousal, making her cry out. In the distance, many of the pack howled as if in response.

"Are you ready for us, mate?" Jace whispered, his mouth flush against her as he flicked his tongue pushing against the spasm of her internal muscles. She whimpered when he pulled away to reposition himself between her thighs.

Jace drew the head of his cock through her essence before thrusting inside her. He pumped in and out again, his strong, measured stokes making her catch her breath. It was just what she wanted, but it still wasn't enough.

As if sensing her need for more, he motioned Caleb to join them, tugging Sara to sit astride him while Caleb lapped at the two of them, using his mouth to pleasure them both.

"More," Sara grunted, and Jace slid out of her pussy, allowing Caleb to take his place. Caleb stoked himself against her, making her growl and push her hips back at him. He gathered her hair into his fist, angling her throat for his kiss and using his teeth to mark her. Caleb pushed himself inside her, his own movements just as powerful as Jace's had been.

As wonderful as their claim was, Sara still felt as though something was missing. "Please, please," she panted again, opening the links between them, trying to convey how she was feeling.

"Don't worry. We'll give you exactly what you need, Sara," Caleb reassured her. He adjusted their position so that Sara was draped over him. She gasped as Caleb thrust back to her and Jace entered her anally. It was as if they had closed an electric circuit.

"This isn't traditionally how the public claiming works." Jace chuckled.

"You can joke at a time like this?" Her muscles clamped down, making both men groan. Sara smiled at their reaction.

"Clearly it's no laughing matter," Caleb said solemnly while he angled his hips so that his next movement dragged his shaft along her G-spot, causing her smile to fade as she was quickly pushed her up over the edge into an earsplitting climax that had the entire pack howling in the distance, welcoming her home.

Epilogue

Ostara, one year later

Sara sat with her back against the large tree in the clearing, letting the power of the tree flow through her in a way she'd been unable to feel when she'd been human. Her son was bundled up, cradled against her chest. The longing she felt to run with the pack was strong, but she was content to sit this one out while she felt the connection to the earth and to her child.

She watched Jace as he spoke with the new council. No longer referred to as the Elders Council, they were now just the Council of Lycan Affairs, and Jace had risen within their ranks once he discovered that members had indeed plotted with the Yellow-Claw Pack, intending to mate her with one of their own.

Now they focused on things that impacted the lycan community as a whole. They were concentrating on interpack relations to stop fighting among the packs so that each pack could prosper. They were also focused on finding the fertility cure, and all packs now shared equal favor among them.

Adian fussed in her arms, and she kissed the top of his head, thankful she had him. It hadn't been an easy pregnancy or birth, despite the fact that they'd conceived so effortlessly. Lycan babies were big, as Jace and the doctor had warned her. She'd spent the last two months of her pregnancy on complete bed rest. Luckily, with two mates and a newly acquired pack that seemed to want to cater to her, she hadn't wanted for anything.

"Hey, beautiful." Caleb kissed her, taking the squirming baby from her arms. "Shh. Daddy's got you." Adian immediately stopped fussing at the sound of Caleb's voice and blinked big dark eyes up at him.

Caleb cooed at the baby, making Sara laugh. "He's got you wrapped around his little finger."

Jace appeared before them as if drawn by the sound of her laughter. "Why don't you go join the pack? We can't have you miss your first Ostara celebration as a full-fledged wolf."

"Yeah?"

"Go. We've got Adian."

Sara stood and then leaned up on her toes to kiss Jace. He gave her a gentle push toward the group waiting to run, and as Sara shifted, stretching out her wolf form, she couldn't imagine life being any sweeter.

Titles by A.R. McKinnon

Friend Zone
Lycan's Mate

* * * *

The FOR MORE Series
Wish List

A.R. McKinnon

A.R. McKinnon lives in southwestern Ontario Most days she can be found at the computer frantically typing out the tales of her characters who won't leave her alone until their stories are told.

She encourages readers to contact her!

Main Web site: https://armckinnon.com/

Twitter: https://twitter.com/AR_McKinnon

Facebook: https://www.facebook.com/ar.mckinnonauthor

Made in the USA
Middletown, DE
15 May 2021

39761815R00109